Stories by Contemporary Writers

MICHELIA

This book is edited and designed by the Editorial Committee of *Cultural China* series

Text by Pan Xiangli
Translation by Kayan Wong
Cover Image by Getty Images
Interior Design by Xue Wenqing
Cover Design by Wang Wei

Editor: Yang Xinci
Editorial Director: Zhang Yicong

Senior Consultants: Sun Yong, Wu Ying, Yang Xinci
Managing Director and Publisher: Wang Youbu

ISBN: 978-1-60220-242-9

Address any comments about *White Michelia* to:

Better Link Press
99 Park Ave
New York, NY 10016
USA

or

Shanghai Press and Publishing Development Company
F 7 Donghu Road, Shanghai, China (200031)
Email: comments_betterlinkpress@hotmail.com

Printed in China by Shanghai Donnelley Printing Co., Ltd.

1 3 5 7 9 10 8 6 4 2

WHITE MICHELIA

By Pan Xiangli

Better Link Press

Foreword

This collection of books for English readers consists of short stories and novellas published by writers based in Shanghai. Apart from a few who are immigrants to Shanghai, most of them were born in the city, from the latter part of the 1940s to the 1980s. Some of them had their works published in the late 1970s and the early 1980s; some gained recognition only in the 21st century. The older among them were the focus of the "To the Mountains and Villages" campaign in their youth, and as a result, lived and worked in the villages. The difficult paths of their lives had given them unique experiences and perspectives prior to their eventual return to Shanghai. They took up creative writing for different reasons but all share a creative urge and a love for writing. By profession, some of them are college professors, some literary editors, some directors of literary institutions, some freelance writers and some professional writers. From the individual styles of the authors and the art of their writings, readers can easily detect traces of the authors' own experiences in life, their interests, as well as their aesthetic values. Most of the works in this collection are still written in the realistic style that represents, in a painstakingly fashioned fictional world, the changes of the times in urban and rural life. Having grown up in a more open era, the younger writers have been spared the hardships experienced by their predecessors, and therefore seek greater freedom in their writing. Whatever category of writers they belong to, all of them have gained their rightful places in the Chinese literary circles over the last forty years. Shanghai writers tend to favor urban narratives more than other genres of writing. Most of the works in this collection can be characterized as urban literature with Shanghai characteristics, but there are also exceptions.

Called the "Paris of the East," Shanghai was already an international metropolis in the 1920s and 30s. Being the center of China's economy, culture and literature at the time, it housed a majority of writers of importance in the history of modern Chinese literature. The list includes Lu Xun, Guo Moruo, Mao Dun and Ba Jin, who had all written and published prolifically in Shanghai. Now, with Shanghai re-emerging as a globalized metropolis, the Shanghai writers who have appeared on the literary scene in the last forty years all face new challenges and literary quests of the times. I am confident that some of the older writers will produce new masterpieces. As for the fledging new generation of writers, we naturally expect them to go far in their long writing careers ahead of them. In due course, we will also introduce those writers who did not make it into this collection.

Wang Jiren
Series Editor

Contents

The Way of Her Fragrance

9:28 a.m. Li Sijin stepped out of the taxi by the entrance of the New Century Press Building. The automatic doors opened smoothly on both sides, and Li Sijin walked in without a pause. The security guard looked up, ready with his usual: "May I please see your I.D.," but stopped as soon as he saw her. Li Sijin did not notice the expression on the security guard's face; in fact, she did not look at him at all. She was full of energy, yet pensive. Her hard-soled shoes clattered across the marble floor, leaving behind a wisp of intense, spicy, and yet thin aroma. The guard, of course, did not know anything about BVLGARI, but he thought curiously: this is not quite the smell of a flower; perhaps more like the taste of ginger.

At 9:30, Li Sijin arrived on time at the office with the glass sign that read "Deputy Managing Editor." She took her seat with timed precision. When she sat down, she adjusted her tan pleated skirt with ease. This maneuver appeared quite practiced; but in fact, she had not practiced it for many years. She had not worn skirts in many years.

Checking the appointment book on the desk, there is a meeting with a Guangzhou newspaper at 10:30. Luo Yi agreed to see them together. He was to arrive around 10:00.

About this man named Luo Yi, Li Sijin would gladly disclose: Luo Yi, Li Sijin's boss, founder and editor-in-chief of *The City Intelligencer*; also the youngest editor-in-chief in the country at the time; a legend in the news world. He was the idol of young recruits in the industry. Just last year, he was interviewed seven times by television heavyweights, and was named "Top Ten Most Valuable People" in the nation. There were countless magazine and newspaper features.

Of course, there were other parts Li Sijin would not disclose. For example, he was the reason she wore skirts. One day, while watching a modeling contest on TV, he pointed to a model wearing a pleated skirt and said, "This girl looks very stylish." The next day, Li Sijin started to wear skirts.

10:00. She heard footsteps outside the door, looked up, and saw Luo Yi standing by the doorway.

He smiled and said to her, "Good morning." Refreshing, as usual.

Li Sijin waved the pencil in her hand, and breezily said, "Morning!" After he walked past, she remembered to check the mirror. Her hair and skin were fine. She breathed a sigh of relief.

10:30. The receptionist from the lobby called. "Chief Li, the client from Guangzhou is here to see you."

Li Sijin said, "Ask them to go directly to the top floor conference room. Send someone to go with them." She dialed Luo Yi's extension. "They're here. I'll go up first. You can go up later."

The chief editors' offices were on the 4th floor. The top floor conference room was on the 20th floor. She pressed 20 in the elevator, and smiled. Originally, it was she who strongly recommended to Luo Yi that the offices of the editors-in-chief should not be above the 5th floor. Luo Yi wanted the 19th floor, but Li Sijin said, "If something happens we can all forget about escaping." Luo Yi, slightly surprised, said, "Why do women always anticipate the worst?" Li Sijin replied without hesitation, "This way things won't end in a total disaster!" Luo Yi finally accepted her suggestion.

The outside world all believed he was omnipotent, but Li Sijin's opinion always had an impact on him. Perhaps since then, she had had wonderful sentiments towards him.

Standing by the elevator on the 20th floor, she welcomed her guests. They were led by the elderly Mr. Zhang, followed by three young people. "How are you, Chief Zhang, long time no see!" When Chief Zhang saw it was her, he said, "Sijin, do you keep yourself fresh in the refrigerator? You are always so young, and you have even grown prettier?" Everyone laughed. Li Sijin invited them to have a seat, and said, "Luo Yi will be here shortly."

In front of clients, everyone at the newspaper called Luo Yi by name. It was forbidden to call him Chief Luo. This was his only command.

There is no seniority in the news business, only merit. This was Luo Yi's famous quote.

When Luo Yi entered the conference room, everyone respectfully stood up. Only Li Sijin stayed seated and quietly watched this man in front of her. Every time she watched him like this in public, his brilliance blinded her. He looked 27, 28, younger than his actual age. At 175 cm, with his thin face, thick hair, slender soft eyes, and refined half-rimmed glasses, he looked like an Ivy League graduate student. But his broad shoulders and assertive gait revealed the truth: here was someone powerful and commanding. Today he wore a pullover T-shirt underneath a semi-casual jacket, and fitted pants; simple and comfortable, and yet respectful for meeting clients.

The first time she complimented him on his style, he replied, "Ruxue bought all of it. The clothes she buys, I can mix and match and it all looks good." Mei Ruxue is his wife. This response turned Li Sijin's first compliment into her last compliment.

Mei Ruxue was just like her name: fair complexion, petite, fragile. She was the extreme opposite of Li Sijin's capable, intense, and graceful character. Li Sijin suspected she was a calculating woman; otherwise, how could she have Luo Yi under such complete control? Several times, she attempted to find a flaw in her. But there were none. She was that simple, that clean, without any opinions, without an edge; a girl without any worldly perspective.

Li Sijin's suspicion turned into envy, with a dash of hurt and hatred. It is a kind of luxury for a woman to remain in that state. Of course, it was possible for Mei Ruxue. She had a husband like Luo Yi and could be immune from being in public. She did not have to work hard and fight in the workplace. At this thought, Li Sijin slid from the peak of jealousy into the abyss of sadness.

In the book *To Be a Woman* it was said: perfection is God's business, not our business. Li Sijin's thirty-two years of life have convinced her to firmly believe this. Mere mortals have no destiny with perfection; if things are too perfect, something is bound to go wrong. Li Sijin had always watched the perfect couple with both worry and anticipation.

And then something did go wrong. At this moment, Mei Ruxue is lying in a hospital bed.

The tragedy that befell Mr. and Mrs. Luo was a car accident. Nine vehicles collided on the highway; Mei Ruxue was in the fourth car in the middle. Her car was hit multiple times, and was crushed like a piece of crumpled chocolate wrapper. Mei Ruxue almost died. Although she was saved, her spine suffered serious injury, resulting in paralysis. Luo Yi took her to numerous hospitals and sought out many renowned doctors, but in the end he had to accept the reality: his wife would never stand up again.

Just like that, the beautiful Mei Ruxue ended up in a hospital bed. Luo Yi's marriage had become a mere scrap of paper.

Mei Ruxue had attempted suicide. Luo Yi said to her, "How could you be so foolish?" Mei Ruxue said, "I know I have to let you go. But without you I cannot go on. If I die, both problems are solved!" Luo Yi said calmly, "You will never lose me. I'm yours forever." Mei Ruxue said, "I don't want to drag you along. It will be too hard for you!" Luo Yi smiled softly and said, "Then that is my life. Let us accept our fate." Mei Ruxue watched her husband for a long time and burst into tears. Luo Yi held her head in his arms, smiling constantly. Finally, Luo Yi said, "Don't do anything foolish again. If you die, I will not live on alone either."

Just like that, as long as Luo Yi was in Shanghai, he would visit Mei Ruxue at the hospital after work, until around 10:00 p.m. He would then go home to rest properly. More than once, the doctors and nurses at the hospital had been moved to tears by their display of affection.

Upon hearing all this, Li Sijin's heart was crushed by a giant pair of pincers. The pain is suffocating, but she could not let it go. She knew: he is finished. Or to put it another way: as far as she is concerned, he could only be an abstract idea.

If Mei Ruxue had not been injured, she would still have a chance. She never believed in those fairy tale lies about love of a lifetime. Even if you were an ethereal angel, as time goes by things grow numb and dull. Luo Yi's career and fame were going through fast changes; it was impossible that Mei Ruxue could understand and accept all of it. If Luo Yi explained it all to her, it would take a long time, and without experiencing it herself, she could never truly understand. Li Sijin believed: at home, Luo Yi was a lonely man without anyone to cheer him on. Mei Ruxue loved Luo Yi, but she could not love him properly; she only loved him like an average husband.

Li Sijin read a quote: "A pasture full of vibrant flowers, but the cattle only sees food." She felt Luo Yi was the poor flowers, and Mei Ruxue was just the pretty cow. As she thought about this, she handed the quote to Luo Yi, along with a venomous smile. Luo Yi smiled too: "I know what you're thinking. To people who don't know how to read, our newspaper is just four-jiao-500-gram waste paper (1 U.S. dime is about 6.1 jiao). But there is deep meaning here too. If we can produce the newspaper with more levels of potential, then those who understand it will see flowers, and those who don't get it will just see feed. This could prove successful for us."

Li Sijin hesitated for a moment, then secretly let out a sigh. This is Luo Yi—Luo Yi with whom she was hopelessly infatuated. No matter what you say, he would think of something related to the newspaper and come up with a great idea. As a colleague, she could only admire and respect him; as a woman, she could only grow more bitter.

How could she fall in love with such a person?

But she also knew; if not such a person, she would find it difficult to really love someone. She only lamented having her sights set so high; now, she is past 30 and still single.

Although the marrying age is growing more relaxed, it is hard not to mind the matter. Other people viewed her as a modern woman who did not care for formal marriage, who must be cohabitating with her boyfriend, a fresh flower not without proper nurture. But in fact, she was truly alone and lonely. But even if she were more lonely, she would not give in easily. Unless there was a man better than Luo Yi, Li Sijin would not be tempted to get married. But after looking around for so long, there was no one better than Luo Yi.

Li Sijin thought she was very objective. But in reality she was suffering the same problem as for all women. As is often the case for women, as soon as she implants someone into her heart, all others become decorations—perhaps even the center person's decoration. Even if Li Sijin were more capable, she is still a woman. So, Luo Yi had become the center of her life and the source of her distress. For him, she refreshed her makeup, wore skirts, donned scarves; she wanted to do more for him, but for now this is all she could do.

After Mei Ruxue's accident, Li Sijin's pain was no less than Luo Yi's. She lamented quietly for herself, and felt pain for Luo Yi. Could he just drag on like this? Besides not being about to take care of her husband or to bear him children, Mei Ruxue could not have a sex life. Luo Yi was just 33; was such a life humane? But the fool never liked the choice of the majority. He had to be different. But this time, the sacrifice for being different is a lifetime of happiness. Did Luo Yi know this?

She was sleepless for several nights in a row. She grew pale, and almost fell sick. Luo Yi noticed, and asked, "Are you tired?" Li Sijin said, "Yes, my heart is tired." She really was tired, because she spent several days deciding whether to give up on Luo Yi.

She felt she had to give up. Because she really could not see any hope. It was like climbing to the top of the mountain alone; there was no more trail other than jumping and being destroyed into pieces. The only choice was to slowly walk back down the same route. Giving up was undoubtedly wise. She looked at the road behind her, and gave a sad eulogy to her feelings from the past few years. But inspiration came just in time. She grabbed the rope, and suddenly swung over to another hilltop.

Luo Yi will have a tragic ending. It will be impossible for him to carry his resolve until the very end—to continuously give without receiving replenishment. He did not run on solar power. After eight to ten years, he is sure to become exhausted. When the pressure pushes him to the limit, he will have a mental breakdown, and then everything will spiral out of control. Perhaps then, a common young female newspaper rookie can conquer him. Luo Yi will start from a place of self-sacrifice, but will end by a simple error. He will let the nameless killer take advantage of him.

She hated that mysterious woman, that shameless bitch who lies in wait in Luo Yi's path. She must make the pre-emptive strike and not let that shameless woman take advantage of the situation, lest Luo Yi's name be destroyed in the process. She could not watch him fall to such a tragic end.

Giving up is not an option. Once she decided, she felt much lighter, like a shell had been shed.

Li Sijin stepped out of the predicament of unrequited love and into the light as a savior angel.

The end of the year quickly arrived, and it was time for the company trip. The privilege to choose the destination fell to the department with the best performance. This year's vote went to the Feature Story department. The Feature Story department was so excited that they came up with too many ideas and no final choice. The department manager's name was Mr. Hao; his nickname was Nice Old Man. Nice Old Man said, "One person should decide, or else we'll be here until next year!" Who should decide? Practically, it should be either the oldest or the youngest. Nice Old Man was the most senior. He wanted to take a democratic vote, so he will certainly abstain. That leaves the youngest, Hai Qing. Hai Qing was a freshman from last year; she had an aura about her, nothing offensive. One of the four princely bachelors at the newspaper, Jiang Liyang, even pointed out that she looked like the actress Zhou Xun. Li Sijin liked the sound of her name, Hai Qing meaning blue water—picturesque and full of vibrant color.

Everyone liked her, so the group all agreed: "Hai Qing should pick! Hai Qing should pick!"

Hai Qing said with a smile, "You really want me to choose? I can't decide so quickly. How about this, let me think about it, and I'll reveal the answer after lunch!"

After lunch, Hai Qing revealed her pick: Jinxi. Everyone wondered: "Jinxi? Where is that?" "Never heard of it."

Hai Qing waved the copy of the weekly newspaper *Shanghai Times* in her hands. "I also just read about it. It's an ancient town along Dianshan Lake. Not many people know about it. There are old bridges, brick kilns, covered walkways; we can drink tea, play cards, eat freshwater fish. This definitely won't cost too much. After dinner we can spend the night in Kunshan. The next day we can have a crab feast."

Nice Old Man said: "Plus we can each bring a couple dozens of them back to Shanghai!"

The crowd approved with a burst of applause and immediately called Luo Yi. Luo Yi said, "Great idea! Announce it on the company intranet." Luo Yi was willing to do this himself, except he never learned how to input Chinese characters on the computer.

Saturday morning, everyone met at the newspaper lobby entrance, then set off.

The two buses were filled to capacity; they set off with excitement. Jinxi was only about an hour from Shanghai. Speeding along Route 318 was relaxing.

Arriving in Jinxi, the group asked Hai Qing, "Where should we go first?" Hai Qing said, "According to the information provided by the newspaper, we should go to the scholars pavilion first." Someone chuckled, "This year, of all things, we cannot believe the newspaper." Hai Qing replied, "Even if others don't believe it, we have to believe it. Otherwise we would be defeating ourselves." Luo Yi laughed heartily. Off to the Scholars Pavilion.

The Scholars Pavilion was quaint with old traditional touches. The people of Jinxi were devoted to learning, and there were many scholars; so this place had become a symbol of prosperous scholarship. In the past, many scholars liked to come here to discuss their works. Li Sijin said, "We should come here to work too." Jiang Liyang said, "Forget it. Newspapers require no scholarship." Hai Qing glanced at Luo Yi and noticed he showed not a hint of anger. She could not help but wonder, for someone so successful, he sure did not put his profession on a high pedestal. Li Sijin said, "At least it's at the edge of cultural tradition." As she said this, she tapped the gong and clasped her hands in a quick bow of worship.

After the worship, Li Sijin looked for Luo Yi. He was not with the rest of the group, but was standing near the window. Li Sijin walked over and looked outside at the dry lotus leaves and wire-like branches, reflecting in the water. Li Sijin's heart tightened; was Luo Yi thinking of Mei Ruxue? She said quickly: "Summer is coming. The lake must be filled with the fragrance of lotus flowers." Luo Yi looked at her; Li Sijin thought maybe she had disturbed him, but she also thought he understood and would not blame her. Sure enough, Luo Yi smiled and said, "This is good too, a more modern composition."

At this point, Hai Qing also hopped over; she looked out the window and exclaimed, "Wow! It is like a painting! A modern ink painting!"

Luo Yi smiled. "We think alike."

Li Sijin felt this girl talked a bit too much. Who do you think you are? We were talking, and you come here with your shouts and screams?

Tea time and cards were up next. Even though Luo Yi did not know how to play, he sat next to the table and watched. Li Sijin was at this table, but so was Hai Qing. Li Sijin felt uncomfortable, and said, "Luo Yi, your standing here is making me lose. Can you go watch somewhere else?"

Jiang Liyang chuckled: "You can't blame others

when you lose. It's not the wind nor sail, it's your heart!"

This was a common joke back at the office. But for Li Sijin it was exactly a matter of her heart. She wanted to fight back, but her face blushed, and she could only pretend she did not hear it.

Someone nearby quickly said: "If your heart desires, then act quickly!" This was in a commercial.

Li Sijin did not dare to look at Luo Yi, and only used her ears to gauge his reaction. He suddenly said: "Why did you play the king and not the ace?"

Hai Qing angrily said: "Don't call it out!" Turns out she had a pair of aces. She guessed her opponent had a pair of 10's. When someone played the 2 of clubs, she only played the king of clubs, to save the pair of aces for beating the pair of 10's.

When everyone heard Luo Yi ask this amateur question, they all laughed. The delicate issue earlier was like a figment of Li Sijin's own imagination. She was secretly relieved, but also a bit disappointed.

After tea, they got up and kept moving. "Everyone please take a look. These are the green blocked bridge embankments and white plastered residences for the locals." Hai Qing imitated the tone of a tour guide.

They all laughed: "Such a sad tour guide!" She said, "I did not make it up. The newspaper said it." Everyone praised the rustic atmosphere, but it was hard to tell whether it was sincere.

In fact, many of the ancient towns near Jiangnan (a region south of the lower reaches of the Yangtze River) were similar; it was all bridges and water, Ming and Qing architecture, rustic, moist, common. Li Sijin did not like this atmosphere; she felt it was all a bit corny, a bit behind the times. If it was for going back to basics, this kind of place was not ideal. Li Sijin liked the city and did not mind the crowds, the pollution, and the human alienation. It is convenient, civilized, and modern. If Li Sijin had to live here in this ancient town, and she could not see the daily national newspapers, or have access to fashion magazines, or have department stores, coffee shops, bars; and she had to wash vegetables and clothes in the same river where others washed their toilets; she would rather someone just kill her. Li Sijin also believed most white-collar workers were like herself: they have already been spoiled by the city, but they could not be honest with themselves. They were just fine living in the city, but they had to insist on escaping the city and returning to the village. Such spoiled children.

Someone like Luo Yi probably does not like this type of place either. There is too little information, too few people, and no room for him to show his talent.

Jiang Liyang said, "Luo Yi, do you like this place? Be honest."

"It depends how you look at it. To live here: definitely not. Day trip: not bad." Luo Yi's answer was surprisingly modest, with no edge to it.

"It's not a bad place for retirement. Make money in Shanghai, and then spend it here; that guarantees a good life at old age." Nice Old Man expressed it this way.

"It's too deserted, don't you think? By then, your daughter won't even come to see you. You'll stare at the water under the bridge every day and grow to think about life's regrets." Jiang Liyang said this but changed subject again to ask, "Luo Yi, have you thought about old age? How will you retire?"

Luo Yi's face turned desolate as if a cold wind blew. "I try not to think about it."

Li Sijin thought: you will not be lonely; you will still have me. You just don't know it right now.

Jiang Liyang then asked, "Sijin, what about you?" Li Sijin replied sharply, "I've thought about it. By then, I will live in a suburban villa with the man I love. We will be a respectable couple with our health and money. We will take strolls on the grass, have afternoon tea by floor-to-ceiling windows, and reminisce about our young glory days. Maybe he'll write a memoir; he'll write a chapter and I'll read a chapter. Occasionally we'll drive into the city to see how our favorite places have changed. We'll have dinner then head back home."

Everyone bursted, "That's great!" "If retirement can be like that, I wouldn't mind being old now!"

Luo Yi's gaze fell on Li Sijin's face; it stayed there meaningfully for a moment, and then moved away. Li Sijin replied with a brilliant smile. Did he hear it? Who is the male lead for the blueprint of her later years?

In Li Sijin's imagination, she had sketched this picture of life with Luo Yi countless times. There were pictures of two people dearly in love, bodies entangled, which made her face blush and her heart race. But, more often, there were vignettes of two people in old age living together quietly and warmly.

For example, Luo Yi would fall asleep on the couch while reading, and she would put a thick blanket on him. Or they would be walking, and her shawl would slip and Luo Yi would fix it ... Why were her thoughts never the two of them young and vibrant, living triumphantly in front of the spotlight? She did not know. Maybe subconsciously she felt that a man like Luo Yi would only truly belong to a woman after he leaves the arena. Li Sijin's philosophy on love was this: all or nothing. She was not afraid to compete with another woman. But she had no confidence competing with his career.

They arrived at Kunshan at night. They had already had dinner, and there was nowhere to go in the small streets, so everyone went to sing karaoke at the hotel bar. All the songs were old, as was the equipment. Everything was idle; they were not so much passing their time as digesting their food. There was a dance floor in the middle; those who did not sing went to dance lazily.

Jiang Liyang asked Li Sijin to dance. Li Sijin said, "Aren't you the young generation? Why do you still do something not trendy?" Jiang Liyang did not explain but just pulled her up. Not only could Jiang Liyang dance; his features were pleasant to look at up close; it made Li Sijin's heart flutter a bit. She moved her gaze to look for Luo Yi. He was watching from the sofa; his look of indifference made her angry, and she leaned deeper into Jiang Liyang's arms. Jiang Liyang adjusted his arms in time, and put more strength in the hand on Li Sijin's back.

It had been a while since she had physical contact with a man, especially a man this young. Young men are nice. His hands were warm, his features were well defined, and his appearance clean and decent. His body emitted a clean, shower fresh fragrance. Maybe because everyone had a bit to drink; Li Sijin's body was especially soft, and her expression carried an unusual helplessness. They danced tenderly through the song. Half awake and half asleep, Li Sijin thought: no wonder he is one of the four princely bachelors. Too bad he was younger by many years, plus he was a player. Otherwise, finding a man like him would be a way to satisfy vanity.

When the song ended, Jiang Liyang held on to her and said softly, "Don't go yet, let's continue." The next song started; it was *Lover's Tears*. The two danced slowly together in the middle of the dance floor. Jiang Liyang said, "Let me ask you a question." Li Sijin answered lazily, "Go ahead." Jiang Liyang said, "The woman in my arms—is this Li Sijin? Or is the everyday Li Sijin not the real Li Sijin?" His breath tickled her ear, and she ducked with a smile.

On the road back to Shanghai, Luo Yi gave Hai Qing his basket of crabs. Hai Qing asked, "How come? You eat it." Luo Yi simply said, "We don't cook at home." Hai Qing said, "Then I won't be shy. Thank you."

Li Sijin thought: you, shy? Those of you born after 1975, I'm afraid the word "shy" is not in your vocabulary.

A scandal began to spread from the newspaper bureau.

Luo Yi was not the first to hear, but he also was not the last. One time, when he sat down at the cafeteria, someone behind him said, "Why not? He's human. It would be more surprising if something didn't happen."

His heart jumped, thinking it was referring to him. But he listened further and realized it was referring to Li Sijin and Jiang Liyang. The "he" was actually referring to a "she." The discussion behind him got more heated—

"Don't assume she's so fierce all the time. Turns out she's quite modern, robbing the cradle!"

"Jiang Liyang's got quite a unique hobby. I heard he fell in love with his teacher when he was little."

"I bet he is willing to sacrifice for his future. Nice Old Man from the Feature Story department is retiring soon. He will undoubtedly become the new manager. He's already become so close with the leadership ..."

"Oh, you make it sound like he is selling out his body. That's disgusting. I had a pretty good impression about him too."

"I don't believe any of it. All I've heard are plot summaries. Do you have any details?"

"Lunch date. Everyday."

"Don't be ridiculous. I don't believe it! They're just having lunch. Doesn't everyone go out to lunch together?"

"What kind of lunch? A love lunch, followed by a quick nap to rest."

"Isn't that a bit rushed?"

"It's a race against the clock. They must be quick!"

"Ha ha ha!"

Luo Yi slammed down his stainless steel spoon and made an audible noise just loud enough for others to hear. The group behind him turned around to look, and stopped with embarrassment.

He did not believe it was true. He was also a bit angry. The two of them—one of them was his deputy, the other was his favorite; why were they so careless to let others compile this kind of news? Moreover it was ugly; to put it plainly, one was unbearably lonely, and the other had an ulterior motive to seduce a female senior supervisor. This was bad for them and for the entire newspaper bureau. He must have a talk with Li Sijin sometime, but she must not take it the wrong way, lest she thinks he was jealous. Getting burned was never his style.

It was time for lunch. Jiang Liyang's face appeared at Li Sijin's door once again. "What do you want for lunch today?" His handsome face smiled like the clear blue sky.

"I don't want to eat anything."

"Not hungry? Then how about curry?"

Li Sijin said, "Come in." Jiang Liyang gave a look that said, "Why?" But Li Sijin insisted. Once he stepped in, she closed the door. Jiang Liyang said, "If you close the door, they'll talk even more viciously!"

Li Sijin ignored his joke and said seriously, "I can't have lunch with you."

"Why?"

"They're already printing gossip about us."

"So what?" Jiang Liyang's face showed he did not care.

"You do not care?"

"Let it be, let it be," Jiang Liyang sang.

"I care. How can I carry this tarnished name? I still have to get married someday."

"Then let's get serious, then your name won't be tarnished." Jiang Liyang was still looking relaxed, as if he was discussing entertainment news.

"You shut up! I hate when you're like this. You're not taking others' feelings into account."

"Why should I care about others' feelings?" After a moment of quiet, he suddenly said, "You're afraid someone might get upset."

Li Sijin could not believe that he knew. She asked, "I'm afraid that who might get upset?"

Jiang Liyang restrained his smile. "Do not think

we're all fools. If I were you, I would not reject this scandal about us. For one, it can be a distraction from the truth; secondly, it can provoke him, let him know there are other men in the world other than him."

Stunned, Li Sijin stared at Jiang Liyang. He knew. He understood everything. This young man was not as heartless as he appeared on the surface. At the end of the day, what role was he playing? What did he want? Would he do something harmful to her or to Luo Yi?

Jiang Liyang said, "Come get curry with me? I'll accept questions."

The two arrived at the curry house across from the Garden Restaurant. Li Sijin endured for a moment, but finally asked, "How did you know?"

"I've watched you. And you're not one to hide."

"What do you want to do?" Li Sijin was nervous.

"Give me ten million yuan (1 U.S. dollar is about 6.1 yuan), otherwise I will tell." Jiang Liyang acted out a gangster extortionist scene from a movie, and then burst into laughter.

Li Sijin relaxed a bit, but kept watching him with suspicion.

Under her gaze, Jiang Liyang finished his medium-spicy curry beef stew. He wiped his mouth and said, "You've stared a hole through me already. OK, I'll tell you. What do you want to know?"

"I don't know how to ask," Li Sijin said honestly.

Jiang Liyang smiled. "Then I don't know how to say it either." He lit a cigarette. Li Sijin noticed he was smoking the "555" brand of cigarettes, the same brand as her father. He smoked fiercely, as if smoking was the whole meaning of his life. Then, like one looking for a faded path in a grass field in the wilderness, he said slowly, "You. Have you thought of this kind of possibility where someone is intrigued by you, and therefore started secretly watching you, and discovered you are completely different from how everyone usually understood you? Then, this person was caught off guard, and could not control himself."

Li Sijin thought for a moment, and said, "But this person will not take this seriously."

"He is serious."

"I don't like to have this kind of relationship with someone working at the same place," Li Sijin continued to reply. Jiang Liyang watched her, shook his head, and thought: look, she is putting on her armor again, except her mouth does not match her heart. This is a completely different woman than the one dancing close to me in my arms.

Li Sijin asked, "Did you hear?"

Jiang Liyang casually put out the cigarette. "Don't tell me he's not your boss!"

Li Sijin said, "I would resign if it means things could work out with him!"

Jiang Liyang showed no sign of weakness. "What's the big deal about a resignation? Isn't it just a job? Waiting for it to mean something before resigning—how old fashioned!"

Caught off guard, Li Sijin did not know what to say; she only stared at him in anger. Jiang Liyang met her gaze and said ruthlessly, "You like him because he's hard for you to have. Does he like you? What has he done for you? What promise can he give you? This is ridiculous!"

Li Sijin said angrily, "So why do you like me? Do you just want to conquer your female supervisor, or just want to tease an old woman?"

Jiang Liyang: "Does a man need a reason to like a woman? I'll forgive anything you say, because you've never been loved deeply."

Finally he added nonchalantly: "If you care

about what others say, I'll resign tomorrow."

Li Sijin felt her whole brain had short-circuited.

Her curry arrived. She had asked for extra spicy, and it should have been very spicy, but at this point she could not taste anything.

She could not sleep at night, and only fell asleep at dawn. She dreamed that Luo Yi was driving with her in the car; suddenly, Jiang Liyang appeared on the road. The car came to a screeching stop; she got out of the car and saw blood all over Jiang Liyang. She said to Luo Yi, "Whatever happens, don't say you were driving! Say I was driving." When the police came, the police took her away screaming ... She woke in a cold sweat. It was only 5 o'clock, so she fell back asleep; when she woke again it was already 9 o'clock. Today, for the first time ever, Li Sijin was late to work. As soon as she arrived at the office, Luo Yi called her to his office.

She went over clumsily. He handed her a sheet of paper; she picked it up and saw that it was Jiang Liyang's resignation letter. A4 size, 80 grams paper, white and crisp, with computer printed text. Just a few lines, wide apart, with handwritten signature in blue—all very much Jiang Liyang's style.

"I had no idea!"

"You've been negligent."

"I ... he and I were nothing, really. I don't know why he did this."

"I don't care what your relationship is! Can it not get to this point? Or, if I can't expect much from you, can you give me a warning next time?"

Li Sijin had never seen Luo Yi so angry; she could not help but feel fear, anxiety, pain, and shame. Her face turned pale white; something caught in her throat, and she took forever to spit out one sentence: "Where is Jiang Liyang?" She wanted to find him immediately and make him take back his letter—no, make him eat it.

"He's in Hainan. He said he needed a long vacation."

Li Sijin suddenly cried.

After Jiang Liyang resigned, Li Sijin fell into a depressed mood.

Originally, spending time with Jiang Liyang made her feel less isolated at the newspaper. At least there was someone to share with, from the heart. But it immediately provoked a series of trouble, and now

Jiang Liyang even resigned. It was not easy to wait for his return from Hainan. She looked for him and found him, but he was not moved; he even said, "Why are you nagging? Have you really gotten old?" Li Sijin had no answer. When asked what kind of work he would look for next, he actually said he did not want to work. He wanted to rest for a few months. He had the tone of someone out of this world. Li Sijin left in anger.

The part that killed her was Luo Yi's disappointment in her. After the last accusations, he had not said much else. But she knew he was very disappointed; his opinion of her had plummeted. The hazy layer of emotional feelings between them had disappeared. The incident had revealed the cold contour of truth; he was the boss, and she was only his subordinate. The loyalty is one-sided; she willfully did everything for him, but he did not have a cent's worth of feelings above and beyond that of a boss.

He no longer stopped by her door every morning; there was no longer the familiar sound of "Good morning!" In public, he looked at her the same way he looked at everyone else.

In everyone else's eyes, she was still his reliable

assistant. But only she knew that they were no longer the closer-than-friends partnership with a certain unspoken understanding.

She swallowed the pain alone and traveled to several different cities for press production and distribution. Even though she did not have to go herself, she felt she had to pay for her crime this year. Her public relations skills are superb; add to that her drinking ability and her soft words, she was practically invincible. Several times, she got herself half-drunk; but even though she drank more and more, she could not get herself any more drunk.

The others said, "You drank an ocean's worth!" She laughed. Where was there an ocean's worth of wine? Only in the bitterness of the heart; it is like an ocean—deep, with no end in sight.

In the past when she traveled for work, she routinely called Luo Yi every day. This time, it had been almost a month, and she had not called him once.

At the last stop of Hangzhou, after seeing everyone she needed to see, she stayed for one more night. In the cool night, the temperature was very low. Walking alone by the water, in the pale white light, she felt like a wandering ghost.

She wanted to keep walking until the end of the world. That way, she did not have to return to Shanghai; she did not have to think of her personal Battle of Waterloo; she did not have to remember the fruitless years of sentiments and emotions. What does Shanghai have to do with me? Without me, it would still go on, business as usual. *The City Intelligencer* will not miss a beat. Luo Yi will continue to be the young talented role model that he is. Who was waiting for me to go back? I will not go back. But if I do not go back, where in this vast world should my body and my mind settle?

Just then, the phone rang. It was Luo Yi.

"Sijin, are you okay? Why haven't you called in so many days?"

Li Sijin wanted to say "I'm fine," but she could not get it out. On the line, Luo Yi said, "Sijin? Sijin?" It sounded so close to her ear, so gentle, with so much care. Tears began to fall from Li Sijin's eyes. She thought, "This man. After all, I can't escape from the palm of his hands."

"There's not much to report. Everything went smoothly," she said, as calmly as she could.

"I understand. When are you coming back?"

"Why should I come back? To listen to you lecture at me again?"

"Sijin, I admit I had a bad attitude that day. But I was that way because it was you. I've always thought that we understood each other. I could not figure out why we were not communicating, so I got a bit anxious. Are you upset with me?"

"No."

"That's good. Come back soon."

Back at the newspaper the next day, just as she sat down in her office, Luo Yi appeared at the door. Smiling, he said, "Good morning!" Refreshing as usual, it appeared he was not too angry or too gentle in his concern. Li Sijin also acted as usual and gave him a sunny smile. After so many years, the two of them often resolved conflicts in this inconclusive manner.

No wonder at the newspaper everyone says Luo Yi and Li Sijin were solid partners—not the romantic kind, but a golden partnership of chemistry and a powerful alliance.

Christmas Eve happened to fall on Saturday. Most

people did not come to work, and the chief editors took turns on duty. This time it was Luo Yi's turn.

The security guard was surprised when he saw Li Sijin at the door: wasn't it Luo Yi who was on duty? Why is Chief Li showing up as well? Of course, he kept his mouth shut as he watched Li Sijin walk in, looking straight ahead. She left behind a new, sweet aroma that was reminiscent of ripe strawberries.

When Luo Yi saw Li Sijin appear at the door, he was not surprised. "You look very nice today. Off to a party?"

Li Sijin dressed differently today. Under her black mink coat was a form-fitting white velvet *chipao* dress that accentuated her curves and her feminine charm. "What are your plans for today?"

"What else can I plan? After work duty, I'll visit Ruxue at the hospital."

"Can't you take just one day off out of the year? Let's go grab a drink." Li Sijin took off her coat and sat down on his desk. She played with the letter opener in his pen holder until she was certain he caught a glimpse of the slit of her dress.

"Sijin, you can find many others to keep you company tonight, but Ruxue only has me and no one else." It was obvious that he was referring not only to Christmas Eve. It was also obvious that, for him, this fact was not without pain. But he kept a smile all the same. Li Sijin had a sudden impulse to lunge at him and tear off his façade.

Luo Yi discerned some danger, so he left his desk, poured a glass of water, and placed it on the coffee table. "Here, have some water." Li Sijin walked over and sat down on the sofa.

Luo Yi turned around and brought back a beautifully wrapped big box. "It's for you. Merry Christmas!" Li Sijin's face lit up as she received the box. She thought: all this time you pretended to keep a distance, and yet you prepared a gift for me! She opened it; it was the year's most popular Swarovski fur collar, embedded with crystals, in tea color. Li Sijin never imagined it would be such a luxurious and intimate gift. Touching the soft fur, she had mixed feelings and did not know what to say.

Luo Yi asked, "Do you like it? I thought it matches you very well, but wasn't sure."

Li Sijin blushed and said, "I like it very much!" She took the scarf out of the box. "Here, help me put it on."

Luo Yi hesitated for a second, took it, walked around the coffee table, and stood facing her. He wrapped the fur around her neck. This maneuver was very much like he was hugging her. Luo Yi moved with jerky gestures; it felt as if he was walking on thin ice.

After he finished this dangerous maneuver, Li Sijin hugged him. She held his waist tightly and buried her face in his chest. She never hesitated, as if she had done this hundreds of times.

Luo Yi wanted to break free, but did not move. He whispered, "Sijin." Li Sijin ignored him, and focused on burying her face into his chest. She wanted to bury all of herself into his body.

Luo Yi made a determined attempt to pull away, but failed. His chest became hot. He closed his eyes and let her breath penetrate his body until his whole being was riddled with a thousand gaping wounds. His heart wrestled with hundreds of ideas and thoughts, like a boat in choppy waters.

Just then, the phone rang, waking them with alarm. Luo Yi immediately pulled away Li Sijin's arm, adjusted his breathing, and went to his desk. After pausing for a second, he picked up.

"Hello, this is Luo Yi. Thanks, and Merry Christmas to you as well. Not much happened today, nothing sudden. Great, I'll call you if anything comes up. Sounds good. Bye."

Luo Yi hung up the phone and said, "That was Hai Qing. She said she was idle today and asked if she could work some overtime." Before Li Sijin could reply, her phone also chimed with a new text message: "Miss Li, Merry Christmas! Stay beautiful! Hai Qing."

Li Sijin could not help but sneer. Luo Yi asked, "Why such a strange laugh? Was it a joke?"

"No. Hai Qing also sent me a Christmas greeting."

"That's nice of her."

"Of course. She's quite fierce."

"Really?" Luo Yi was surprised.

"You don't think so? Everyone likes her. She flirts relentlessly; men or women, no one is immune."

Luo Yi laughed. "That bad?"

"Of course you don't think it's that bad. You obviously like her."

"Me? That's not possible."

"Really? Are you willing to swear you've never

been tempted by her?" Li Sijin was unwilling to let it go.

Luo Yi regained his usual composure. "You really don't know me then. How could I, with someone at the newspaper?"

After he said this, it was impossible for the two of them to return to the atmosphere of their embrace. Li Sijin was disappointed, but she was also reluctant to go. So she waited until his shift was over, then drove him to the hospital and watched him walk into the dark entrance of the inpatient department. She slowly leaned onto the steering wheel. She wanted to cry, but she could not.

Her original plan for the night was all or nothing: either the two of them would spend the evening together in harmony, or it would end in utter rejection. But the result was neither. Luo Yi's gift clearly showed that he did not view her as a boss viewed a subordinate; he did not view her as simply a friend. And yet he was resolute in his intentions; even though he did not pretend to be a saint, he was able to draw a clear boundary like a river, and Li Sijin was relegated to the opposite shore. Perhaps he was not being truthful, but it was a warning to Li Sijin: do not move forward, or you'll be doing so at your own risk. This state of being neither dead nor alive was not exactly the Christmas present that Li Sijin had hoped for.

Luo Yi said to Li Sijin: "The circulation numbers for next year are out; it's 70,000 copies more than last year." These days, the newspaper business was extremely competitive. It was difficult for most newspapers to keep circulation numbers from sliding. For *The City Intelligencer* to have numbers go up, therefore, was quite impressive.

Li Sijin fixed her gaze tenderly on Luo Yi. "With you here, everything is possible." This was the truth from her heart, and it was because of this truth that she was willing to stand by his side, to the death, as his loyal right-hand woman.

"Don't say that. If I hear too many compliments, it'll cloud my thinking. Your circulation campaign was very effective. There haven't been any rewards for you." "That's right, how will you reward me?" "I want to send you on a holiday abroad. You can check out some media agencies for us along the way."

Li Sijin shouted with joy: "Really?"

Luo Yi just smiled in silence.

Thinking quietly for a moment, Li Sijin said, "I

don't want to go abroad. I want another reward."

"What?" Luo Yi was a little surprised.

"On the last day of the year, I want you to come with me to Long Hua Temple to ring the bell and burn incense. Okay?" Her tone was completely prayer-like.

Luo Yi's first reaction was: no, of course no. But considering her hard work, plus the sorrowful look in her eyes at this moment, it was impossible to refuse her. He was at a loss for words.

"Go with me. We'll eat the vegetarian fast, ring the bell, burn incense, and make our wishes. We'll spend a night at the temple. I've already booked the room." Seeing Luo Yi was still speechless, she smiled secretively: "You do not dare to go because of the room, is that right? Don't worry; it will be two single beds. Besides, we won't be sleeping. We can chat all night. It's a temple. No one will indecently assault you. The deities will blame me. I don't want bad luck all next year!"

At the mention of "indecent assault," Luo Yi laughed. "What kind of a world do we live in when a woman promises not to assault a man!"

"Go. I listen to you 365 days out of the year. You can't even listen to me once?"

Luo Yi finally replied, "Okay, Sijin." His voice was like velvet.

The next few days, Li Sijin felt the sky was exceptionally blue, and the sun was exceptionally bright. She felt incredibly light; with every step, she wanted to twirl and skip.

At the moment right before the start of the New Year, Li Sijin was finally at Long Hua Temple with Luo Yi. They listened to the 108 rings of the gong that resonated through the crowd's bodies. Li Sijin quickly clasped her hands together and bowed her head to make a wish. She was being extra devout; not only did she stuff several hundred-yuan bills into the collection box, she actually knelt down at the altar to offer the first incense.

Luo Yi smiled and watched from the sidelines. When she got up, he asked, "So devout. What was your wish?"

"Do you want to know?" Li Sijin looked far away. Her face and her voice were both as ethereal as the night fog.

Luo Yi regretted asking, so he only said, "It's cold outside. Let's head back to the room."

They returned to the room and turned the

heater on full blast. They took off their coats and their sweaters, and drank tea and chatted away. Li Sijin said the sofa was too cramped. She walked over to the bed, hopped in, and leaned back. "This is more comfortable." Luo Yi went to the other bed and sat cross-legged. They stared at each other and could not help but laugh.

Luo Yi said, "The world of scandal is incredible. If someone found out we shared a room at Long Hua Temple, who knows what kind of story they'll spin. No one will believe the truth; even I feel like it's a lie."

Li Sijin said: "If it were anybody else, I wouldn't believe it. But our Luo Yi is different. If it's you, I'd believe it."

"Don't make me out to be a saint. Everyone knows it's difficult to come down from a pedestal," Luo Yi said, laughing.

"Oh, you're not a saint? Then I know, there must be some other reason."

"Come on! Don't mess with me with your sympathy. I'm not a eunuch!"

They laughed hysterically together. When they stopped laughing, each stared up quietly at the ceiling. Neither spoke.

Li Sijin asked, "Do you know what I wished for earlier?"

Luo Yi looked at her and said nothing. In his eyes were pity and a bit of helplessness.

Li Sijin's face glowed as if she was dreaming. She said in a sing-song voice: "I want to be with you."

Luo Yi sighed. "I know."

"You know?" Li Sijin asked, sitting up.

"I'm not a fool." Luo Yi walked over and sat down beside Li Sijin. He asked solemnly: "When you say you want to be with me, do you mean at home, or at the newspaper?"

Li Sijin said without hesitation: "Both."

Luo Yi lifted her face and looked closely. He brushed aside a wisp of hair and said, "Sijin, don't make it difficult for me, okay?"

"How is it difficult for you?"

"You're asking for too much. I cannot give it." He was still smiling when he spoke, his voice still like velvet.

Hai Qing became the star of *The City Intelligencer*.

There are two standards for evaluating the workload of the *Intelligencer*'s writing staff. First is the monthly writing quota; the second is the ratio of well-received assignments. This formula dictated each month's bonus for each reporter. Also named are the quarterly star reporter and the annual star reporter, announced each quarter and at the end of the year.

Being a star reporter not only solidifies the position at the newspaper, it usually comes with substantial rewards—including a five-figure bonus. Selection of the star reporters is a major event and big news at the newspaper.

For two consecutive quarters, Hai Qing was selected as the star reporter. She was not the only one who had been selected for two consecutive quarters, but she was the only one selected by unanimous vote. That is to say, even Li Sijin gave her the vote of approval. They both came out of the news business and understood the fight and the struggles involved, so there was admiration for her hard work. Luo Yi also praised her at the company-wide business meeting. He also said the news business requires natural talent; without natural talent, hard work and effort are wasted—you may as well change careers as early as possible.

Watching Luo Yi lavish praise, and seeing Hai

Qing grow thinner but still full of energy, Li Sijin thought, maybe this girl truly is made for the news business. When I was her age, I did not compare. She also thought, someone so talented, Luo Yi must not be able to help but love her. If I think too much, I would just appear petty and lose face. At this thought, her usual discomfort subsided.

Everyone in the department insisted Hai Qing take them all out to dinner. Hai Qing graciously agreed, and even asked Nice Old Man to notify Luo Yi and Li Sijin. Li Sijin agreed to attend when she saw Luo Yi also agreed to attend. Unexpectedly, something came up on the night of the dinner and she could not go. She phoned Luo Yi from the road.

"It's that cosmetics company that wanted to advertise with us for the whole year. We haven't heard from them in forever, and now all of a sudden they appear again. Yes, it's a big fish. I can't go to Hai Qing's dinner."

"That's fine, she's our own people." Luo Yi's voice was pleasant.

"That's right. It's ok if I don't go, as long as Your Highness the Editor-in-Chief shows up." Li Sijin said this with a bit of mischief.

"Come on! I'm not going either. Two articles need to be put together today; they are still being written, and I have no idea when they will be done for me to see the proof. No sympathy from you, just sarcasm." Luo Yi seemed to be in a good mood too.

"Is that right. It seems a bit insincere to say we would go and then not show up. Do you think Hai Qing will be upset?" Li Sijin tried as best she could to not show her gladness.

"She wouldn't be so petty, right? No matter. At least you will all have dinner at nice places. I just have the cafeteria."

Li Sijin said, "What's good to eat in the cafeteria? I'll call takeout for you."

"No need to order takeout. Since the client is taking you out, order extra dishes and ask express delivery to send me the leftovers."

Li Sijin laughed heartily. After she ended the call with Luo Yi, she immediately called a 24-hour Hong Kong cafe and ordered a crispy roast goose dinner combo for delivery after 7:30 p.m. She knew Luo Yi loved roast goose. She also knew that if it was delivered before 7:30 p.m., the proof most likely will not be ready, and Luo Yi will definitely not eat until it is done. Once roast goose goes cold, it is not as tasty.

The next day, soon after Li Sijin arrived in her office and started checking her email, there was a soft knock on the door. It was Hai Qing. Today she wore a white cotton shirt with jeans; she looked like a young, innocent student. Li Sijin noticed her right collar was not folded neatly.

Hai Qing said politely, "Miss Li, good morning!"

"Hai Qing, come on in, the door is open."

Hai Qing smiled and walked in quietly. She stood with her hands folded, and only sat down gingerly when Li Sijin asked her to do so.

Li Sijin poured her a glass of water, and said, "I'm sorry about last night. I had to meet with an advertiser client. It was unexpected."

Hai Qing said, "Aiya, Miss Li, you don't have to be so cordial with me. Of course I understand."

Li Sijin smiled and sat down across from Hai Qing to hear why she stopped by. Unexpectedly, she handed over a paper bag. "Dinner didn't happen, so this small gift will have to do. Miss Li, you must accept it."

Li Sijin hesitated, then smiled and received the

gift. Inside the bag was a beautiful box; in it were beauty soaps and signature body treatments from The Beauty Soup Hot Spring and Spa. Judging from the packaging, the gift was not cheap.

"Hai Qing, you didn't have to, I ..."

Hai Qing looked into her eyes, and said very earnestly: "Miss Li, I know that without you I would have never been star reporter. I know you don't expect anything in return, but I am sincerely thankful for you."

Li Sijin did not expect her to speak so directly, and her heart was warmed. "Hai Qing, you didn't have to say that. This is all because of your hard work. But I will accept your gift gladly. Thank you."

It all seemed too serious, so she added: "Besides, I need to pamper myself and pretty up a bit, or else I'll turn into an old hag."

Hai Qing also eased up and said, "Miss Li must be joking. You are pretty and full of style. They're all saying it behind your back, but you're the real flower of the newspaper."

"You're kidding. How come I've never heard that before?"

"Who would dare to say that in front of you?

If you don't believe me, ask our director." Hai Qing spoke with extra seriousness.

Li Sijin had never heard this kind of talk. Her heart was secretly happy, but her lips said, "Even if I'm the flower, I'm about to wilt, unlike you, still vibrant and full of life."

"We're not flowers. We're just grass. I see it very clearly: at the newspaper, aside from you, Miss Li, we are all a field of grass."

Li Sijin laughed; for the first time, she realized the young lady was adorable. When she walked her out of the office, she could not help but reach out and fix Hai Qing's collar.

But things quickly started going wrong.

In the pitch summaries from the Feature Story department, she discovered a plan for a 3,000-word story on hot springs. The summary described the recently popular trend of hot springs and their benefits for beauty, health ... She thought about Hai Qing's gift box from The Beauty Soup. Could it be ...? She thought for a moment, shook it off, and signed her name as approval.

Three days later, the draft arrived at her desk. Hai

Qing was the author. The draft was clearly marked "urgent," which meant it required priority attention. It was fine before Li Sijin read it; but as soon as she read it, she gasped.

On the surface, the story described hot springs and spas from Japan to Southeast Asia. But the focus was entirely on introducing The Beauty Soup. From the cultural perspective, to effectiveness, to current trends, every paragraph used The Beauty Soup as an example. The "Historical Context" section should have described the history of hot springs; there should not be any reference to beauty soups. But no, it actually said the Huaqing pool from Tang era Chang'An was the most renowned beauty soup, with a poem to prove it: "Water from the hot spring washes creamy smooth." This was not a reporting piece; it was an advertising editorial for The Beauty Soup!

She knew nothing would come out of asking Hai Qing. But if she asked Nice Old Man about it, she was afraid of wrongly accusing anyone and spreading bad vibes in the process. After some thought, she decided to give The Beauty Soup a visit herself. She discovered that this well-known beauty spa salon used to be a bathhouse. But because of an injury accident involving electrical leakage, business grew cold. After a change of owner, the business now focused on spa and beauty, along with a line of popular bath and treatment products. This year was their fifth anniversary, with a celebration happening next month. The owner was advertising in the major newspapers and television stations, plus handing out bonus prizes to promote the business.

Pretending to be a customer, Li Sijin quickly became chummy with the assistant general manager, who assumed Li Sijin was a wealthy housewife and, thus, showered her with extra attention. Acting like a confidante, she recommended a specially priced VIP card to Li Sijin—prepay only 2,000 yuan for a card that was worth 3,500 yuan. "If you will be coming in anyway, this is a great deal." Li Sijin replied, "Then reserve one for me." She followed by earnestly saying, "This place is really good. I hadn't heard about it. It seems you haven't advertised much." "That's right. Our boss is pretty angry about it. He's ready to burn some cash and play this up."

Li Sijin casually said, "Why not do a promotion with *The City Intelligencer*? A lot of people read that newspaper." The young assistant manager said, "We already did." Li Sijin pretended to have the inside scoop: "Advertisements are not effective enough. Get a reporter to write an editorial. They're not that expensive, maybe 3,000 yuan for a full page."

The assistant manager said, "What? Their female reporter came last time and asked for 5,000 yuan! We've been had! No matter, we have not paid yet. When the time comes, we will not hand over the money so easily! I have to speak with my boss about this. People are so corrupt these days. That young woman, she looked so calm and nice. Who knew!"

Back at the newspaper, Li Sijin dialed Hai Qing's extension. She was not there, so she called Nice Old Man and simply said, "We cannot use the spa piece." "Why? I thought it was pretty good. Should we let Luo Yi take a look?"

Li Sijin sighed at his naiveté and said, "I've already decided. When Hai Qing returns, ask her to stop by my office."

Hai Qing returned in the afternoon. She was dressed differently, this time wearing a tight fitting pleated shirt and a long skirt with tropical fish pattern. Li Sijin suddenly realized that, last time, Hai Qing had prepared to come see her and had carefully picked out an outfit for it.

Li Sijin closed the door. She noticed Hai Qing's face was slightly pale.

Li Sijin asked, "Do you know why I've asked to see you?"

"No, I don't."

"Tell me. How did you decide to do that piece on The Beauty Soup?"

"That article was about hot springs." Hai Qing calmed down and corrected Li Sijin with an academic tone.

Li Sijin smiled coldly, walked back to her seat, and sat down. She stared at Hai Qing with a sharp gaze.

Hai Qing pondered a moment, then asked, "Is there a problem?"

Seeing how she had the nerve to ask this question, Li Sijin went into a rage and blurted out, "Let me ask you this. At 5,000 yuan per page, aren't you selling our newspaper a bit too cheaply?"

Hai Qing's face grew more pale, but her voice remained calm: "I don't know what you're talking about."

"You don't know? Okay, I will hold a company

wide meeting, you can explain to everyone!"

"Miss Li, let me explain. They did make the offer, but honestly I have not taken a single cent. I wrote the article because I felt it was a worthwhile topic."

"Of course you have not taken a single cent. You're waiting for the article to be published before receiving your compensation, isn't that right? No wonder you've been so dedicated. It's their anniversary celebration; the timing is impeccable! What are you doing with our newspaper?"

"If we're going to write it either way, might as well do them a favor. It doesn't hurt us. Didn't Luo Yi say it's best to make more friends in the news business?"

"Don't bring Luo Yi into this! He hates sellouts. Let's see how he reprimands you once he finds out!"

"You're deliberately setting me up! He won't believe you!"

"Correct. He will not believe me, but will he believe you? This is good. I want to see just how much he trusts you!"

Li Sijin rushed to Luo Yi's office. He was on the phone, and gestured for her to take a seat. She glanced at the sofa but did not sit down, and instead stood across from Luo Yi. As soon as he finished the call, she said, "Someone is selling editorial copy. Do you want to be involved?"

"Who?"

"Hai Qing!"

"Are you sure?"

Li Sijin went through all the details from start to finish; she even proposed to use Hai Qing's gift box from The Beauty Soup as evidence. She handed over the article: "Look, advertisement for The Beauty Soup throughout the article."

Luo Yi took it, read over it carefully, and even made notes on it with his red pen. "It goes a little too far in some spots. Ask her to change them and it will be fine."

"What? She sold a whole page of content for 5,000 yuan. If we don't take care of this, others will copy. How will our newspaper go on like this?" Li Sijin was simply mad at this point.

"What did she say?"

"Of course she admitted to nothing. What thief would admit to being a thief? Isn't this obvious? Do you still have to ask?"

Luo Yi furrowed his eyebrows. "Sijin, Hai Qing is still young. She doesn't understand the seriousness of this. We'll have a talk with her and she'll understand. If we discipline her, how can she do her job afterwards?"

"What are you talking about?" Li Sijin simply could not believe her ears. Is this Luo Yi? The one who lives for the news and holds integrity and principles above all else?

"Don't be upset. I'll take care of this. I'll talk to Hai Qing and find out the details of what happened. If there's not much to it, I'll remind her to be careful in these situations so they don't lead to more trouble. This article is a good subject matter. There's a 7-day holiday coming up, and hot springs are a good vacation option; there should be many readers. I'll ask her to fix it." There was not a tinge of anger in Luo Yi's tone.

This drove Li Sijin mad: "Luo Yi, how can you cover for her to this point? Where are your principles, your sense of right and wrong?"

"Sijin, it's not so much principles or right and wrong. She is a good talent. You're the leader, you have to accommodate."

"You're saying I don't know how to accommodate? She sells page space. Not only do you not care; you're now lecturing me? Luo Yi, I never thought …"

Li Sijin was trembling and could not continue. She knew that male leaders were often much more lenient and much more caring towards young female underlings, but she always thought Luo Yi was an exception. But now, the facts in front of her clearly said: Luo Yi is one of those men, a mere mortal!

"Forget about this incident. You don't have to manage it," Luo Yi said, seeing Li Sijin's eyes welled up with tears.

Li Sijin was not the last person to walk out of Luo Yi's office crying. An hour later, when Hai Qing walked out from Luo Yi's office, her eyes and the tip of her nose were also flushed red. No one knew what Luo Yi said to her. But since then, Hai Qing worked extra hard, and her stories and articles became more and more captivating. People were convinced of her abilities.

Luo Yi knew he had completely gained back this young girl. He could now truly utilize her.

There was a small meeting in the company conference room. Apart from a few veterans, there was also Mr. Hao from the Feature Story department. The main topic of the meeting was choosing the next head of the Feature Story department.

Nice Old Man was retiring. He announced his candidates for his successor. None of the names were ideal, but there were no other choices.

Luo Yi asked, "What do you all think of Hai Qing?"

Everyone was slightly surprised. Li Sijin felt like a loud noise had slammed into her head. She nervously looked at Nice Old Man, who pondered a moment, and said, "It's not impossible, but she has not been in the newspaper for a long time. Would she …"

"This is not necessarily related to the length of time at the paper," Luo Yi said.

Nice Old Man said, "Based on her performance, she was our star reporter last year. And she's been re-elected two consecutive quarters this year."

Another vice president said, "Originally, Jiang Liyang was a suitable candidate."

Li Sijin glanced at Luo Yi and caught his gaze looking at her. Her face blushed, and she looked down.

Luo Yi said, "We have no questions about Hai Qing's ability to do the job. She has a quality that I value highly. On the night of 9/11, several of us worked overtime at the paper to write an extra feature. From beginning to the end, Hai Qing exhibited high energy. By the next morning, we couldn't do an extra feature, but she still handed me eight edited pages and said, 'I believe out of all the papers, we are still the best!' After that, with a pale face, she went home, without a bit of complaint. I believe she will be an outstanding newsperson, because she is passionate about the news!"

After hearing this, no one objected. Li Sijin thought: why didn't you mention her phone call to you on Christmas Eve? Passionate about the news ... she's passionate about you! She even sold our editorial space! But she did not say anything at the time. After the meeting, she walked right behind Luo Yi and followed him into his office. She immediately said, "I don't agree."

Luo Yi made a gesture that said "please tell me more."

"At the least, she attempted to sell editorial space, showing an utter lack of ethics. How can such a person be promoted?"

"Don't mention that incident again. I trust Hai Qing. Now and into the future, she will never again have this problem. She has talent, she has passion, that is the most important."

"I don't refute she has passion for her work. Anyone with ambition will have passion. But can she be a leader based on this one trait?"

"Ambition is not such a bad thing."

"Everyone is older than her. How will she be convincing?"

Luo Yi asked: "We have plenty of people older than us under us. How are we leading them?"

"It's not the same! She cannot be compared to us!"

"Why not? I think she compares to us quite well! At least she clearly knows what she wants. She knows when to let things go. She won't let her subordinate lose his job because of a silly scandal!"

Li Sijin never thought Luo Yi would bring up old wounds. She angrily shouted, "Don't slip up, or else you will get mixed up in a scandal with her! By then, maybe you will be the one who fails! I see this little girl is not the pleasant type!"

"If she can cause me to fail, then I will gladly let her go ahead. I'm willing to gamble and I'm willing to lose!"

"Do you realize you've lost all sense of logic? If you want to make a mistake, make a better one. Why do you insist on betting on such bad merchandise!"

"How can you say this? It's unbelievable!" Even Luo Yi started to raise his voice.

"You can't stand it, can you? Talking about the apple of your eye like this."

"Please do not get the job and feelings mixed together! When I evaluate someone, I leave out my personal likes and dislikes."

"Forget it!" Li Sijin finished and slammed the door on her way out.

She found Hai Qing. She asked her, "You worship Luo Yi, don't you? If you're promoted to the head of the department, but the decision affects Luo Yi's future, would you still accept the appointment?"

Hai Qing's face waned for a moment. She asked, "Why would it affect Luo Yi's future?"

"Because it's too unconventional, and everyone will start to suspect your relationship."

"When Luo Yi first promoted you, did people have that reaction?"

Li Sijin gave a cold chuckle. She really was not the pleasant type. "Do you think you and I are the same?"

"No, not the same."

"How so?"

"I don't think complicated like you do. I have no interest in your relationship with Luo Yi. I admire Luo Yi only so that I can learn from him."

"Does this mean you must accept the assignment?" Li Sijin's voice turned into a hiss, like a profuse gas leak.

"As for that, I would only answer when Luo Yi poses the question to me." Hai Qing had regained her entire composure.

Enough! Enough!!! Li Sijin was going 120 km/hr on the highway. She crossed the Nanpu Bridge, and drove madly along Century Avenue. Her heart was a burning wildfire.

When the scenery in front of her eyes became unfamiliar, she realized she needed to go back. On the way, her heart was still filled with unwillingness to accept. Without paying attention, she drove to a hospital entrance. She looked at the hospital sign and realized this was Mei Ruxue's hospital. It's during work hours. Luo Yi would not be here. Why did I come here? Did I want to see Mei Ruxue?

This idea was like a bolt of lightning. It gave her

body a jolt, and her mind, a flicker. Yes, I shall go see Mei Ruxue!

If she doesn't find her, it will be too late. Luo Yi will be finished. She, Li Sijin, would also be finished.

With her reporter I.D., she was able to quickly find out Mei Ruxue's room number. She opened the door, and there was Mei Ruxue.

Mei Ruxue's body was thin, and her face had grown pale. But she looked very far from death. Seeing Li Sijin, she smiled with some doubt, then said, "Hello. Please have a seat."

Li Sijin did not sit. She must take advantage of the ball of fire in her chest and say what she came to say before the fire is extinguished. If she sat down, she would involuntarily smile and express concern. They would slowly begin to chat, and normal human behavior would rein her in; she would then have to retract her claws and all hopes of tearing open a resolution would be lost.

"How long do you plan to torture Luo Yi?"

Mei Ruxue shuddered, as if these words were a knife, suddenly stabbing into her body.

"I do not understand what you mean." She

whispered, like a guilty defendant making her final denial.

"For each day you drag on this marriage, Luo Yi has to live one more day of overloaded burden. How long do you expect him to last? Five years? Ten years? He's a human being, not a god. He is already showing signs of abnormal behavior, and it's because of his abnormal life. He has begun to lose the ability to distinguish women."

"Are you saying he has a girlfriend?" Mei Ruxue said, her eyes covered with tears.

"He doesn't! But there is a terrible woman scheming for him, and he is about to fall for it. It's all because of you. If you hadn't tortured him like this, and made him break down, why would he be like this? Why haven't you left him? You know his responsible nature, so you use him, and make him sacrifice his whole life for you? You are too selfish! A man cannot live without his cause, not to mention this is Luo Yi! What will you get once he's completely ruined? By that time, he will hate you!"

Her anger was like a turbulent storm, and Mei Ruxue was like a wilted leaf, shivering pitifully on a branch.

Finally, as Li Sijin was leaving, Mei Ruxue asked behind her: "You love him, don't you?"

Li Sijin paused. She did not know how to answer. In the end, she left without answering.

Luo Yi had a divorce. This shocking news shook the entire newspaper bureau.

Mei Ruxue went to the United States to get treatment and planned to never return. Her sister lived there. Before she left, it was uncertain how she convinced Luo Yi, but they completed the divorce procedures. The news came from the Civil Affairs Bureau, so it had to be true.

Luo Yi did not appear to change much physically. If it had to be something, it was that his depression, which he had already exhibited, ran a little deeper. Many reporters came to interview him, and vehemently insinuated about his private life. Luo Yi invariably replied in his tired, hollow tone: "There's not much to say about my private life."

Li Sijin's mood was more complicated. She felt conflicted, not knowing whether Luo Yi knew that she had stopped by to see Mei Ruxue. If he knew, god knows what would happen. She was also disappointed; she had desperately hoped for Luo Yi to get divorced, but now that it is reality, it was less satisfying than she had anticipated. Of course, it was a little sweet, but the sweetness was buried beneath the bitterness and the sourness.

She also never had a chance to show him tenderness. The two of them have not been crossing paths lately.

After their big fight over Hai Qing, Hai Qing never took the promotion. Li Sijin felt comforted. But after Nice Old Man retired, the Feature Story department was without leadership, and so Luo Yi took over the responsibilities himself. This was clearly not a permanent solution, and Hai Qing was still slated for the position. The only person subjected to pressure was Li Sijin. She obviously knew this was Luo Yi's plan to make her surrender, so she blatantly feigned ignorance.

Her mood was never sunny. After all, she had gotten into the current state of affairs with Luo Yi over a little rookie girl; she realized she had lost a battle. But it had already happened; there was no use getting upset over it. She began to lose weight, inadvertently shedding several kilograms.

When work was almost done for the day, she received a phone call. It was Jiang Liyang, who had disappeared for a while.

"Where are you now?" Li Sijin asked. She still cared for him.

"It doesn't matter where I am. The important thing is, you seem to have progressed."

"What progress?"

"Seems there's hope of becoming Mrs. Luo, or have you become that already?"

"What are you talking about? We're the same as before."

"In that case, Luo Yi still hasn't worked up the courage to accept you? Or does he in fact not like you? Sijin, I say this man definitely has problems. If it's not physiological then it's psychological. This fine woman right in front of him, and yet he's indifferent. When will you give up on him already?"

"What does this have to do with you?"

Jiang Liyang laughed. "Don't always state the obvious. You know what it has to do with me."

Li Sijin said angrily, "You shut ..." but the phone hung up, leaving her with just the busy tone.

She thought for a moment, and called him back.

"Let's meet. We have to talk."

Jiang Liyang said, "We can meet to talk about private matters. No talk about affairs of the state."

"Who wants to talk about affairs of the state? There's no presidential election; the affairs of the state have nothing to do with us."

"The affairs of *The City Intelligencer* are the affairs of your state. It's Luo Yi's kingdom."

Li Sijin heard this and froze for a moment. Why hadn't she thought of it before? This is Luo Yi's kingdom. Kingdom. Then who was she, and who was everyone else? Her undying loyalty—was it Luo Yi's command, or her own stupidity?

When she saw Jiang Liyang, she spoke her mind. "Liyang, come back. The Feature Story department has no director, and we're very anxious."

"You've lost weight. Has Luo Yi mentioned to you that you've lost weight?"

Li Sijin was caught off guard and did not know what to say.

"Must be a no then. That bastard."

Li Sijin did not want to hear him talk about Luo Yi like this, so she returned to her train of thought. "I really hope you will come back. We really don't have anyone, it's very urgent."

"You're worried, aren't you? Doesn't Luo Yi have someone in mind already?"

"What have you heard?"

"Just because I've left doesn't mean I don't know anything. My people skills are not that bad."

Hearing this, Li Sijin understood that he knew everything and she did not have to hide anymore. "If you don't come back, Hai Qing will get the promotion!"

"Like I said, that's Luo Yi's kingdom, it has nothing to do with me."

"You ... I can't take this anymore! Consider it a favor to me. At the last discussion, someone mentioned your name; Luo Yi also praised you. Only you can block Hai Qing now! I cannot bear to watch her succeed!"

"You despise her so much; is it as supervisor towards an underling, or as a woman towards another woman?"

"It's all the same. When I see her, I can't breathe."

Jiang Liyang could not help but laugh out loud. "Sijin, I advise you to give up. Right now, you're at a bit of a loss. Who are you actually upset with? Hai

Qing or Luo Yi? Why are you opposing Hai Qing? Are you afraid that she is incompetent, or are you afraid she will have many opportunities to be close to Luo Yi? You're setting up quite a battle maneuver— who are you fighting?"

"It's all the same!"

"Not true. If you're upset with Luo Yi, you should speak with him directly. Otherwise, if you oppose Hai Qing like this, you will only lose points in Luo Yi's eyes. Is that what you want?"

Discouraged, Li Sijin said, "I cannot reason with him."

"Then let it go."

"Let what go?"

"Game over, stop playing games. Your influence on him ends here. Do you still not see it?"

"Nonsense."

"Denial again! You keep denying what you cannot accept. This is unrealistic. How can you fight Hai Qing like this? She thinks clearly."

"He used to listen to me. But now ..."

Jiang Liyang made a timeout hand gesture. "Please stop right there. I don't want to listen to any more foolish talk. What do you mean listen to you? You're the one that's been listening to him. You continue to get along, because you keep obeying him. Now that you finally choose to not obey him, and you realize the chemistry is gone. Everything is changed."

Li Sijin listened, paused, then slowly said, "You have watched us like this all along?"

Jiang Liyang nodded. "Your relationship was never balanced. He takes advantage of your feelings for him."

Li Sijin watched the man in front of her eyes—a man several years younger than her—with infinite sadness, infinite bitterness. She was unable to say anything.

Seeing her like this, Jiang Liyang was a little regretful of his heavy-handedness with the matter. But he only wanted her to see it sooner. He did not say any more, and looked down to read the menu. He thought: she's lost so much weight. What should we eat?

Luo Yi did not bring up the subject of Hai Qing's promotion to head the Feature Story department, and neither did Li Sijin. But the members of the department were anxious, and they finally raised the issue at the chief editors' meeting. Luo Yi looked over at Li Sijin; Li Sijin said: "You decide." And just like that, Hai Qing became the head of the department.

Not out of cooperation, but out of tiredness.

She did not want to fight anymore. She did not want to fight over the work or over Luo Yi. Actually, it had been over half a year since Luo Yi's divorce, but he was still aloof about her; in fact, he was sometimes extra cautious around her. Now that there was no real obstacle stopping them, he seemed to have imagined one in his mind, in case Li Sijin just wanted to throw herself into his arms.

Jiang Liyang was right: did he love her? Had he ever loved her?

Public opinion also made her sad. No one ever suspected anything between Luo Yi and Hai Qing, because no one would believe that someone in Luo Yi's status would commit the offense of getting involved with small potatoes. Li Sijin blamed herself for being so stupid as to make Hai Qing into an imaginary enemy.

Some felt that a diamond class bachelor like Luo Yi would never think about remarrying; freedom was precious, and freedom meant limitless possibilities.

Others saw Luo Yi as a traditional man who probably would marry again. His comings and goings with any woman became topics of gossip. The newspaper bureau spent all day discussing his latest girlfriend; sometimes she was a model, sometimes she was a pretty novelist, other times she was an internet CEO. Even though it was all hearsay, the gossip proved that Luo Yi had infinite possibilities. And inside this broad possibility, perhaps there was no room for Li Sijin.

She always thought Mei Ruxue was blocking her way. But now Mei Ruxue was gone, she realized there was never a way to begin with. It was a wide swath of wasteland in front of her.

Li Sijin kept going to work, kept being punctual, and kept leaving a trail of sweet fragrance. But only she knew her steps grew heavy, her eyes grew tired, and she could not focus. She had no appetite. She was not sleeping well; without looking in the mirror, she knew there must be panda-like dark circles around her eyes.

Jiang Liyang frequently came to see her, saying he was bored, and that he needed her care and warmth. He said, "What are we afraid of now?"

Coincidentally, Li Sijin did not want to go home alone, fearful she might not be able to handle her emotions. So she almost always agreed to meet him.

At the bar, they acted like two of the most professional, most dedicated drinkers. They drank with concentration, going from bar to bar. Sometimes they commiserated over being the forgotten ones in the world. They sighed and comforted each other. Other times, they could not stand the sight of each other. She scolded him for being a good-for-nothing, for not doing something with his career. He scolded her for ruining her life over a man who did not love her, and that she was the real good-for-nothing. They would get angry, and Li Sijin would hit him. He did not block her punches, and kept drinking in between her blows.

They spent most of their time repeating pointless nonsense.

"Jiang Liyang, what's your Chinese zodiac animal?"

"You want to ask for my age? Don't need to be so subtle."

"If I wanted to know your age, I don't have to ask you. I can just look up your company profile."

Jiang Liyang said, "I know you're my former boss. There's no need to remind me."

"Don't change the subject! What's your animal?"

"I'm year of the rabbit."

Li Sijin said, "Ahh, you're five years younger than me!"

"You're a bit boring; one little thing and you can think it over and over again. So what if I'm five years younger?"

"It feels strange. I used to never give the time of day to any man younger than me, not even by one year."

"So now that you're spending time with me, then what? Is lightning going to strike? Are you going to die? Shoot!" Jiang Liyang said disdainfully.

Li Sijin ignored him. She just kept looking around, and noticed the leftover reindeer stencils on the window from Christmas. She thought aloud, "Liyang, don't you think the twelve zodiac animals are strange? Why did they include the fictional dragon, but omitted the deer, which actually exists?"

"It used to be included. The ancient Yunmeng Qin tomb bamboo texts had a section called *The Book of Days*. In it, the twelve zodiacs included the deer but not the dog. The zodiac signs were not set in stone from the beginning; they went through phases of change. For reasons unknown, the dog later replaced the deer. As for the dragons, they were part of ancient totem worship."

Li Sijin had always known that he was an expert in foreign languages and computers, but she did not expect him to have knowledge on piles of old books. In her thoughts she respected him, but in words: "Then why isn't there a phoenix as well? Aren't the dragon and the phoenix always together? Or were they being sexist?"

Jiang Liyang knew she was deliberately being a troublemaker, so he retorted, "Have you forgotten your cultural knowledge already? The phoenix is male; only the fire phoenix is female. The famous poem song by Sima Xiangru was called *Phoenix Yearns for the Fire Phoenix*. The phoenix is male; the fire phoenix is female!"

Li Sijin was speechless, so she simply offered a toast: "Let's drink to that. I respect you." Jiang Liyang laughed heartily, exposing his bright white teeth. His eyes sparkled like black onyx.

Li Sijin thought, what a handsome man. Also,

he is quite outstanding. He would not simply find a woman to hold him down; he should not. As for herself, she has no time to play emotional hide and seek with men. When she was young, she thought there would be plenty of suitors, and that she would have to selectively choose one to marry. Why has she fallen to this state of affairs? So much time, passed in vain. No—it all but drained away, like a spring in the desert, flowing and evaporating into thin air.

All because of Luo Yi!

When Li Sijin gets drunk, she cries. She weeps on the table, on the bar. Jiang Liyang rarely got drunk, because he had to take Li Sijin home. They both drive—she in her secondhand BMW, he in his brand new VW Polo. But when they meet at the bar, they never drive, because after they get drunk they had to call taxis.

One night at 3 a.m., on the way home, Li Sijin said, "Jiang Liyang, why do you have patience to spend time with me?"

Jiang Liyang knew she was drunk, so he did not answer; he only asked the driver: "Can you turn down the A.C.?" Even thought it was spring, it was still chilly at night. He worried she might catch a cold from the temperature difference inside and outside the taxi.

Li Sijin would not relent and kept asking, "Jiang Liyang, say it, why do you have patience? Tell me, tell me."

"I don't want to say it."

"Why?"

"You won't believe me even if I told you."

Li Sijin laughed. "Just say it. I'll believe you. I am the most trusting kind of person. Whatever people tell me, I believe it, especially if it's from someone so handsome."

The driver could not help but laugh too. Jiang Liyang said, "What are you laughing at?" He then said to Li Sijin, "You're drunk. Stop talking. Go to sleep, we're almost there."

"Go to sleep, to sleep. So tired, tired ..." Li Sijin said as she leaned on Jiang Liyang's shoulder and fell asleep. Her long hair fell all over him, her body rising and falling as she breathed. Her scent rose from her body, warm from the drinks and fragrant from her perfume. It caused him to drift. Suddenly, he remembered the first time he saw her; it was her hyacinth scent that captivated him, that suddenly made him feel infiltrated.

The driver hit the brakes abruptly, and he quickly held her with his arm, to stop her from falling. Watching her stay asleep after that jolt, he realized she must be very tired. No one would let her peacefully go to sleep at night; Luo Yi could not do it, and all he could do was keep her company and let her rest in her stupor. This way of living, this way of being tortured, when will it end? He did not know.

As if she knew what he was thinking, she shook her head several times, then childishly bore herself deeper into his arms.

Jiang Liyang held her softly and stole glances of her quiet sleeping face, the shadows of her eyelashes. He put his lips next to her ear and whispered: "You like me, you just don't know it. Right?"

He said it so quietly that he was not saying it to anyone. He was saying it to himself.

"Sijin, I'm leaving," Jiang Liyang said on the phone.

"Leaving? To where?" Li Sijin was in her office having a headache over a pile of edits.

"Chengdu."

"Ah. For vacation? Is it a trip from there to Tibet or something? How many days?"

"Not for vacation. I'm moving there."

"What? You're kidding."

"It's true. I'm at the airport now. I wrote you an email with the details. I have to board the plane now. Goodbye."

And the phone hung up. She called again but his phone was already off. Li Sijin quickly checked her inbox, but the connection was extremely slow. She kept anxiously clicking the mouse and chaotically pressing on the keyboard until the inbox opened. She found Jiang Liyang's email; the subject was "I'm not sure if you would be happy." She immediately read the message:

"Sijin, I've never emailed you before. Today is the first time. Emails feel so distant; it feels like we are very far apart already. It's such a bad feeling. I wanted to tell you face to face; in fact, I wanted to tell you last night, but in the end, I'm not sure why, I could not do it. I really have no way of telling you face to face: I'm leaving.

"A newspaper in Chengdu offered me a job to be executive deputy editor. They offered it a while ago already. But I have been dragging on the decision for the past few months. I wanted to know if I should leave you during this time. They thought I was stalling to negotiate a higher salary, so they almost doubled the offer. Under usual circumstances, it would be irrational to refuse this offer. But that is not why I decided to leave.

"I have never said it, but you should know that I would do anything for you, as long as I am capable. But these past few months, I realized I could not do anything for you. I could only drink with you and listen to you talk about your sadness over and over again. Watching you writhe in pain, despair, jealousy, and self-pity; I cannot change the situation. I cannot watch any more. If I keep going on like this, I would pity myself too, because my existence has no effect on you.

"You keep thinking I'm too young, that I don't understand you. You even think I'm not trustworthy. But they are all excuses. You never faced my feelings directly. Sijin, sometimes I wondered if I'm really that terrible, without any trait that might move you? Did you ever feel I was pestering you? If so, then you must be relieved now. I'm going far, far away, and no one will pester you anymore.

"But if that is not what you think, then don't blame me either. Forcing myself to leave you is a tremendously difficult thing. For that, please forgive me for any way I might have offended you.

"But I am only leaving, not giving up. I will go there, do well at my job, and find a good home. This way, if one day you are willing to be with me, then there will be a warm home waiting for you. This is what drives me as I move to a strange place to start from scratch.

"You have more than enough time to consider and to make a decision. Rest assured. Didn't you always say I had a lot of patience?

"I only ask one thing: if anything happens, or even if nothing happens and you just want to talk to me, for God's sake, call me immediately. My phone will be on 24 hours.

"Liyang"

Li Sijin stared and stared. She felt like her whole being had been tossed into the sea. She was floating aimlessly, uncertain of sorrows or joys, losing her sense of direction.

She pulled the scrollbar on the screen back up,

looked again, then said chokingly: "Jiang Liyang, you bastard!"

Li Sijin walked to the cafeteria. The lunch rush had long passed; there were only three or four people in the cafeteria. Luo Yi was there, sitting alone at a table in the corner. Holding her tray, Li Sijin hesitated for a second before walking over.

Luo Yi smiled at her: "You're eating late."

"I'm too lazy to wait in line."

"Me too. No patience."

Li Sijin smiled and said, "Maybe it has nothing to do with patience. Nobody wants to wait, knowing there's nothing good to eat at the end of the line."

"That is true," Luo Yi said.

Recently they rarely spent time alone together. And when they do bump into each other, it was always cordial, like two acquaintances who had just met—a man and a woman, carefully maneuvering and paying attention to propriety.

After eating silently for a while, Luo Yi asked, "The May Day labor holiday is coming up. Are you going anywhere?"

"I don't know yet. This seven-day holiday is

always tough to handle. At least for New Year's there are things to do. For May Day, staying at home is boring, but going out means dealing with crowds."

"It seems most people like to go out and join the crowd."

"I agree. Sometimes I feel the May Day labor holiday should be called the May Day travel holiday."

Hearing her say this, Luo Yi smiled. Looking at his smile, with his eyes narrowed, she remembered the first time she met him years ago. He was smiling like this, shining like the sun into her life. But, as she got closer to him, she saw the sun less and less.

"Luo Yi, these days, are you doing well?"

Luo Yi hesitated and answered, "Very well."

"Do you have a girlfriend yet? Everyone is spreading small leads, but I want to hear it from the source."

Luo Yi did not expect her to be so blunt and direct. He was caught off guard and could not dodge in time, so he replied frankly, "If you're asking about someone I would settle down with, then no."

Li Sijin said, "I understand." In other words, there was a girlfriend. Moreover, he did not feel the need to explain himself to her. Li Sijin thought: that's strange, why do I not have the urge to jump and kill him? Honestly, she did not have that feeling, not the slightest impulse to do so. It was like this had nothing to do with her; sitting here with Luo Yi, it was like they were chatting about the weather.

A person can easily hurt you, often because you handed him the knife and pointed the blade at yourself. Now, she had tossed the knife aside. She should tell Jiang Liyang about this thought; it would make the guy happy. He might ridicule her, but in his heart he would be very happy.

Just when she thought about calling him, her phone rang.

"Sijin, it's me."

"What a coincidence, I was just thinking of calling you."

"Really? Have you eaten?"

"Yes."

"How are you spending the May Day holiday? Come to Chengdu?"

Sijin remembered what he said last time about preparing a nice, comfortable home for her. He must have ulterior motives. Her face got hot. "I won't come!"

"In that case, does anyone need me to return to Shanghai?"

"Shanghai is a big place, how should I know?"

"You are so not clever. Even if you don't ask me to come back, I'd come back. I set it up for you and you can't even just welcome me? Seriously!"

"Then come back." Before Jiang Liyang could shout for joy, she quickly added, "Shanghai welcomes you!"

This was the slogan on the entrance seen as you come out of the airport.

April 30, the last workday before the 7-day holiday. Office hours had long ended, but Li Sijin was still working overtime. She was taking a pre-emptive strike; she decided not to be on editor duty over the holiday week, so she had to finish all the work on her hands.

These seven days, with Jiang Liyang here, she can thoroughly have a good time and drink with delight. There may be more, but she had to wait until she sees him. With Luo Yi, she always had to initiate. But with Jiang Liyang, she could wait for his lead.

Her phone rang. A look at the caller I.D., it was Jiang Liyang.

He must be calling to let her know his arrival time tomorrow. She answered with a smile, "Liyang, do you have your ticket yet?"

Jiang Liyang's voice sounded a bit strange—more abrupt than usual, and in a lower tone. "Sijin, I'm on the plane."

"That's fantastic. You're coming in early. Did you want to surprise me?" Suddenly, Li Sijin realized something was wrong. "Are you crazy? Why are you using your cellphone on the plane?"

"Sijin, there's a problem with the plane. The landing gear is stuck."

Li Sijin jumped. "What did you say? Don't scare me!"

"After the plane took off, the landing gear could not retract. We've been circling for two hours."

Li Sijin heart leapt into her throat. "Then ... then does that mean you can't land?"

"They made contact with ground control. There must be a way. I have to hang up," he said.

Suddenly, Li Sijin felt she was on a bed of fire, her internal organs heating up, her body emitting smoke. Her brain was like a broken record, spinning over the same spot.

Something's happened. Something's happened. Something's happened. Something's happened. Something's happened.

He said they were thinking of a solution. A solution. A solution.

There must not be a solution. Otherwise, why is the plane still circling? How long can the plane keep circling? Once the fuel runs out, isn't it over?

Tears pierced her eyes. But she mercilessly wiped them away.

She dialed the phone number for the airport, but it was busy. She dialed again and again, but it was busy. She got up, grabbed her coat, rushed to the elevator, went to the underground garage, and drove her car out in a few quick spins. She sprang like a frightened snake and sped towards the airport.

Her phone rang again. It was Jiang Liyang!

She turned on her headset without slowing down her driving speed. "Liyang, tell me quickly, what's happening now?"

"We're still circling. Sijin, do not worry."

"How can I not worry? Why do we encounter such things? Why does it have to be you? What did we do wrong? Why is god doing this to us?" She bit her lip and refused to cry. Don't cry, don't cry, it is too ominous. Liyang will touch down safely. Nothing will happen to him. Nothing. Nothing!

Jiang Liyang's voice had returned to calm. "Sijin, do you remember something I said to you before? To love something fragile is to understand that we can lose it at any moment. Ceramics, sentiments, life. Life is fragile, Sijin."

"You won't! Liyang, you won't!"

"We're running out of fuel. Looks like we will do a forced landing. Promise me, if they show what happens to our plane on the television, don't watch."

"Liyang!" She felt like wailing.

"You must not cry. Whatever happens, for me, you must not cry." Jiang Liyang's voice was near, as if he was whispering gently against her cheek. Except he was on a troubled aircraft. He could be smashed into pieces at any moment!

"Liyang, don't die! I won't let you die! You can't abandon me! You can't go back on your word!"

"Sijin, if I had lived to 80, who knows what would've happened? At least this way I can be certain: at the end of my life I still loved you."

It was like a steel claw had cut rows of wounds

across Li Sijin's heart. She had never felt so much regret. "Liyang, in fact, I never wanted to reject you. I just never felt I deserved you!"

"Sijin, you're so silly. But I love you, you silly woman."

"What did you say?"

"I love you."

Li Sijin wailed. Her violent sobbing sent her body into convulsions. Her mouth stretched wide open, breathless. A flood of tears like countless leather whips slashed her face.

Jiang Liyang's home in Chengdu turned out quite lovely. There were fresh flowers everywhere: balcony, living room, the den, bedroom; in pots, baskets, vases. There were roses, lilies, lotus, quince, hyacinth ... they brightened the entire home, like a jewelry box full of gems that had been turned over, scattering precious stones everywhere.

When he came home, Li Sijin was busy in the kitchen. She heard his movement. She turned around and saw him, and said, "You're home early today."

He did not say a word, but walked over and held her, burying his head into her neck. He stayed there for a long time. Li Sijin laughed and nudged him: "What?" He said, "Just now a sudden fear struck me: that when I open the door, I would not see you here. That it was all a dream that you are here with me, right next to me."

Li Sijin lovingly lifted his head, kissed him on both cheeks, then kissed his lips deeply. Still kissing, Jiang Liyang lifted her up and walked into the bedroom. Li Sijin protested feebly, "Don't you want dinner first? The food will get cold." But Jiang Liyang put her onto the bed and mindlessly started kissing her all over her body. Prompted by the warmth of their body heat, the surrounding flowers began to exude a stronger fragrance. The aroma seeped into their hair and skin. Li Sijin looked at the ceiling with misty eyes, and thought: God, why do I want him so badly like this? It's like I've waited a hundred years.

When the two of them returned from the intoxicating fragrance back to reality, Jiang Liyang said, "You smell very nice. What perfume are you wearing today?" "I didn't use perfume today." "Then your scent, at this very moment, is my favorite."

In the end, the airplane incident did not result in a disaster. The aircraft was able to land, and Jiang

Liyang and all the passengers were able to evacuate via the emergency exit inflatable slide with no injuries. Mentally, they all experienced a trip through hell. Physically, on the other hand, their suffering had a comedic element: in order to prevent an explosion, the fire brigade had sprayed a thick layer of flame-retardant foam on the ground. As the passengers slid down to safety, they each descended into a thick cloud of foam, which covered their heads and their faces.

Li Sijin said under no circumstance would she allow him to fly to Shanghai again; she said if he dared to fly, he can forget about seeing her again. The very next day, she hopped on the first flight to Chengdu. When she saw Jiang Liyang, she ran to him, gave him a few good punches, then cried in his arms. At first, her crying was like an avalanche. Then she cried intermittently; she would sob, look at Jiang Liyang, quiet down for a while, think about what happened, and cry again. In the end, exhausted, she collapsed into Jiang Liyang's arms and slept as if in a coma. Her face was swollen from crying. She even sobbed in her dreams. Jiang Liyang held her tightly, heartbroken.

Luo Yi had never shown this particular facial expression before: that of someone dreaming, but awoken by a needle prick, only to be confused by everything in front of his eyes. That was the precise look on his face when Li Sijin announced her resignation.

"May I ask what this personal reason is?" His tone was a bit slow. When Li Sijin did not reply immediately, he added, "After all, we've known each other for so many years. Can you tell me?"

"My boyfriend is there," Li Sijin replied.

The spark in Luo Yi's eyes shrank suddenly. "For you to do this, is he worth it?"

"Do these types of questions have right or wrong answers? If I feel it's worth it, then it's worth it. If not, then it's not."

"Have you made contacts for jobs? Still want to do newspapers?"

"I don't know. I want to stay at home for a while. All these years working, I'm tired."

"Have you really decided? No more considerations? After all, you're already 32 years old, not fresh out of school like ten years ago. Don't make an impulsive decision."

"I'm 33. Because I'm 33, I don't get too many chances to make impulsive decisions. I want to cherish the opportunity." As Li Sijin spoke, her face revealed a mischievous smile.

Luo Yi gave a long sigh as he leaned back on his chair. "In that case, I can only say: best wishes to you! If things don't go well, come back anytime."

Li Sijin smiled. "I'm going now. I have to pack."

"Will we meet again? This isn't the end, is it?"

"Hard to say. We've had enough of each other for ten years."

Luo Yi replied with a forced smile. When she reached the door, Luo Yi blurted out, "Wait!" He walked over and stood in front of her. After a moment of silence, he said, "Now, you're no longer my colleague." He wrapped her into his arms. Li Sijin was not surprised. She frowned a little, but quietly let him hold her. Then, she softly pulled away, gave him a smile, and left.

When Luo Yi came to, he looked out the door, but she was already gone. The entire hallway was completely empty.

Jiang Liyang never mentioned Luo Yi. Li Sijin could not contain her curiosity and asked him, "Don't you have any questions about me and Luo Yi?"

"Are there any questions I should be asking?"

Li Sijin thought about the times they used to drink together and how she revealed everything to him. She was embarrassed, and asked him deliberately, "Don't you want to know how far we got?"

Jiang Liyang said, "You had guts but no strategy. He had intentions but no guts. How far could it have gone? Fortunately, it's only emotional infidelity. Otherwise he would be dead by now, and not in one piece at that. But you did it."

Li Sijin added, "So you don't care one bit?"

"Care about what? At this point, he's not jealous of me; should I be jealous of him?"

"But in the past, I really liked him." Li Sijin retreated guiltily.

"In the past ... When did you meet him? In 1992? God, I was only 17 at the time, still underage. I can't blame you. I can only blame my parents for having me too late."

Jiang Liyang subscribed to a lot of newspapers for the home. But Li Sijin never thought he would order *The City Intelligencer*. He said, "Reading it is like seeing an old friend." Li Sijin smiled, knowing that he did it just for her.

One day, she saw Hai Qing's name with the title "Deputy Managing Editor" in front. Li Sijin liked to listen to music at home. Today she heard a *pipa* solo piece called *Hai Qing and the Swan*. It had a strong melody, evoking an atmosphere of fighting and seizing. As described in the song introduction, the piece is also called *Hai Qing Seizes the Swan* and is related to hunting in the Mongolian culture. Hai Qing, also called "cyan of the sea," is a type of eagle.

When Jiang Liyang came home, Li Sijin looked a bit entranced. He asked her what was on her mind. "I was wrong. Her name does not refer to the color of the sea. It's a bird of prey."

After waiting for Jiang Liyang to understand what she was referring to, she pondered deeply. "Actually, it's fair. Everyone gets his wish. Everyone has his own way of living, his own gain and loss."

A few days later, he asked, "Sijin, do you want to go back to work?"

"Ha! You can't afford to feed me. I can eat less."

"I'm serious. You've been staying at home. Aren't you bored? Besides, I feel guilty watching you cook and do laundry every day. You're Li Sijin, not an ordinary little woman."

"I know exactly who I am. I'm comfortable at home. When I want to go back to work, I will."

"If you wish, coming to our newspaper would be best. I'm not willing to see you go somewhere else."

Li Sijin imitated him and made a timeout gesture. "Surrender to you? Never. Even a donkey knows not to trip in the same place twice. I'll find a respectable bureau on my own, send in my resume, and wait for word. You stay out of it, you hear me?"

Seeing Li Sijin restored to her former self at the mention of work, Jiang Liyang laughed and said, "Yes!"

Li Sijin continued to read *The City Intelligencer* every day. Sometimes, spotting an error, she would grab a red pen out of habit and mark the error; realizing it was not her job anymore, she would laugh at herself. Looking at the newspaper, she often remembered so much that had happened in the past. But it was like listening to someone else discuss her past life. It was distant, and incredible. She could not understand why that woman from the past was so desperate, so exhausted from trying so hard, so full of hostility.

She also discovered something interesting: reading the same newspaper from the comfort of her sofa at home was very different from reading it in her big swivel chair in her old office. Which one was better—she did not know. She only knew that, back then, she would meticulously put on makeup and apply a variety of perfumes. Now, her face was exceptionally spotless; and on her body, there was only the light scent of fresh flowers.

White Michelia

The car had just come to a stop when Xu Yi jumped out first.

A few seconds later, everyone in the car heard her scream, "Oh, it smells so nice!" He could not help but smile, because of her childishness. She must be 27, 28 already, but still very childish, both in manners and in appearance.

Conceptually speaking, he did not like innocent, naïve women, because acting younger often gives the impression of less intelligence; besides, most of the time it was faked. To fool the eyes of a man his age was not only bad form but usually futile. But she did not know; even if she knew, she did not care—at least that was what he believed. Those born in the 70's, as long as they are happy, no one else mattered.

After they all got out of the car, they took a good look at the resort hotel. It was a lakeside building complex. The lake was expansive like the sea. The water had the unique color of highland lakes. In the distance, there was a lone island, lush with trees. It was a perfect painting in its entirety—nothing could be added or subtracted.

They were surrounded by trees and flowers. The most prominent was a giant white michelia tree. Blossoms filled the branches, giving off an endless, thick sweet aroma. It was overwhelming; being wrapped in it was intoxicating. The aroma was truly "striking," complete with its unique strategy: first it soaked your hair and your clothes, then it penetrated your breathing; as soon as you relax, ahh, the aroma takes over your body internally.

Originally, Ji Mengbei did not want to come to this writers' conference. After so many years as a professional writer for the creative studio, he had attended so many writers' conferences they were becoming annoying. Attendance meant working up a cheerful demeanor for small talk and drinking boring wine. Being over 40, disdain for these events grew year after year.

He realized some people used these conferences to discuss a variety of literary business—book releases, public relations, literary debates, and many other ways to make a buck. They were irrelevant to him, ever since day one of writing.

Legend had it that the conference produced many love stories. There were numerous writers who were trailed by several scandals, but Ji Mengbei did not have any. Many people wondered how he managed to stay immune; others felt sorry that such a handsome man was so unromantic; still others just plain said it was impossible. It was all because he kept his guard up very tightly. To all gossip, Ji Mengbei only smiled. It was not impossible; he just was not interested. He did not want to become the male lead in these rumors, only to get tumbled with the dirt when the crowd talked trash. Whenever he heard his peers being talked about behind their backs, he was always filled with mixed feelings of puzzlement and sympathy: two perfectly good people, why did they not protect themselves better, why did they allow themselves to be treated so badly?

A month ago, the Provincial Writers Association, of which he was a part, had a re-election. He was a strong favorite for one of the positions; in the end, however, he did not win the vote. Originally, he did not care much at all for the position. But since everyone had talked it up as a sure win for him, he was frustrated when it did not come through. It had nothing to do with not getting the spot. He was frustrated because it was not his business to begin with; but then everyone made it his business; and in the end, nothing came of it. It made him look bad. Even if he was not the best candidate, he never wanted to be compared with the others. But somebody had nothing better to do, and caused his innocent humiliation. People who cared about such symbolic titles kept badgering him about the injustice of the situation. He did not want to be disrespectful; but when he agreed with them, the acceptance of the situation was hard to swallow. So he finally decided to escape from it all, and to attend this writers' conference, which he had originally decided not to attend. The conference would be a good break for him!

For Xu Yi, this was her first time at a writers' conference. She has worked at her publishing company for several years, but never had a chance to participate in the conference. This year, the president of her company was supposed to attend. But an important meeting held him back, so he let her come. She was not given any specific assignment other than to get acquainted with some of the writers. What kind of assignment was this? It was more like a glorified retreat for her. Not to mention the conference was in beautiful scenic Yunnan. She was extremely grateful to her boss for giving her, the youngest and most junior staffer, this reward in disguise.

Yesterday, after registration, they spent the night in Kunming, then arrived in Chengjiang. There were a total of nine people attending this conference, the majority of whom were seniors. Of course, they were famous well-known seniors. One of them was Mr. Hu. Xu Yi had read his essays in high school textbooks. Everyone called him Old Hu.

There were also two middle-aged women whose names were well known as well. The two of them talked amongst themselves and never paid Xu Yi any attention. She thought maybe it was because she was not an author. But later, she observed their same behavior towards others, and concluded this was their norm.

Only one of the men was younger than the rest of the group—Ji Mengbei from the army. Word was that he became a colonel at a young age. Since he was in civil service, he did not wear a uniform. She took a few glances at him. He had well-proportioned facial features, glowing wheat-colored skin, and tight lips that looked like they might leak inappropriate comments if opened. He did not show many expressions, and his manners were very discreet. He was not wearing a uniform, but he may as well have been, with his meticulous manners and discipline. In her heart, she secretly called him colonel.

When everyone got off the bus, and the fragrance of the white michelia trees surrounded them, she blurted out, "Oh, it smells so nice!" Afterwards, she felt a bit embarrassed; perhaps they would laugh at her for making a big deal out of nothing. But then she thought, so what? Xu Yi's belief was that putting pressure on yourself based on the opinion of others is an old tacky habit from the last century.

When she looked up, she encountered Ji Mengbei's calm eyes. She could not decipher the meaning behind those eyes; she only knew they saw black and white, as if he unintentionally saw and understood everything.

They had dinner in the hotel restaurant. In addition to a wide variety of fish, there were many delicacies. And because mushrooms were in season, there were specials with porcini, chanterelles, Yunnan mushrooms ... The mushrooms were prepared in numerous ways: stir fried plain, stir fried with peppers and shredded pork, stewed in chicken soup, etc. The mushroom dishes covered half the table.

Xu Yi had never eaten so many different types of fresh wild mushrooms. They were fragrant, fresh, tender, and soft. She ate and ate to her heart's content, trying all the dishes along with three bowls of rice. The only other person at the table who had an appetite like hers was Ji Mengbei. But instead of drinking the soup, he only drank the alcohol.

Old Hu said, "Leave it to the young ones with their good appetites!"

The two middle-aged women—one had the surname Duan, the other Lin. Ms. Duan said, "She is so lucky. Naturally slim, no diet necessary!" Ms. Lin said, "You don't need a diet either!" Ms. Duan smiled. Neither of them was fat.

Xu Yi smiled but did not respond. She heartily finished her bowl of matsutake and bamboo fungus chicken soup before putting down her spoon, fully satisfied.

"Mengbei, let's head over to the lake in a little

bit?" Old Hu said, picking his teeth. "We haven't seen each other in three years."

"Sounds good. I'll come pick you up from your room," Ji Mengbei replied respectfully. Old Hu and Ji Mengbei's father were old friends.

Ms. Duan immediately chimed in. "It's worth taking a walk by the lake. The water is quite beautiful."

Ms. Lin said, "I'll have to lose sleep again tonight. Every time I visit a scenic place, I lose sleep." Xu Yi thought, this little middle-aged woman, I'll call her Little Miss Lin.

So everyone ended up at the lake. They walked in twos and threes; some smoked, some joked, some sang folk songs. Ji Mengbei and Old Hu chatted about what had been going on since they last met, and asked about mutual acquaintances. Both remarked they did not have specific assignments for this trip. Neither of them had to network for business or write any promotional materials. They could truly relax.

Xu Yi picked at the plants as she walked. She held a white michelia in her hand, and smelled its fragrance as she walked.

The air was clean, fragrant, with not a speck of dust. The water in the lake was so pristine, it was unreal. The lake was right under your feet, but it seemed distant. Looking farther, the colors of the water made your heart skip a beat. It was like a mystical legend had just ended, but the sounds still lingered; or perhaps something unusual was about to happen.

The clouds in the sky were plump. They were especially white, especially big; they seemed close by,

Indeed, it felt like a misty fantasy, but the misty fantasy also felt real. Underneath it all, this was such a strange place.

Hearing the group boast about the lake, Old Hu had a thought. "The water of Dianchi Lake does not compare to the water here. Dianchi is too contaminated, and the lake has shrunk. But the old classic epic couplet based on it really was spectacular—'For five hundred *li* Dianchi Lake approaches, as a blanket gathers at the shore, joy filling the boundless skies ...' I can't remember the rest." (one *li* is about 500 meters)

Ji Mengbei remarked, "The fact is, this couplet starts off very well, but the rest of it basically explains the beginning, all for the sake of breaking the record for number of words in an antithetical couplet. For the first line you quoted, the matching second part is: 'Memories of the last thousand years return to my heart, as the wine is finished, sighs wonder where are the heroes.' It's very clean." Old Hu smiled, hesitated for a moment, and said, "That is one way to put it, that is certainly one way to put it!" Xu Yi wondered if he was agreeing or otherwise?

Chatting leisurely like this, Ji Mengbei felt his unpleasantness at the beginning of the trip had simply melted away. His mood lightened. Those petty wins and losses looked very distant now. It was not worth mentioning, not worth his attention, not even worth a flash of thought.

Their guide for the conference, Lee, was about forty years old. His looks were unremarkable; but as soon as he opened his mouth, he showed his intelligence. He waited until everyone had thoroughly enjoyed the view before sharing the legends of the lake.

He said the lake had formed over 3,400,000 years ago. During the Song Dynasty it was called Luojia Lake; common folks called it Herring Playing with Moon Lake.

Old Hu cheered, "Herring Playing with Moon, what a great name!"

Ji Mengbei said, "That's like if a person was called

Li Fengqiu at school, but at home they called her Xiao Lian." Everyone laughed.

Xu Yi thought, Xian Lian, must be a stunning beauty.

After a while, Lee said that that was right, that was the sense. But we can't put it quite as nicely as you have.

When Xu Yi arrived in Chengjiang, she immediately noticed that the people of Chengjiang had a unique character about them; they were unusually gentle and humble. Now, she noticed their tone of voice was also very unique—slow, but not sluggish, as if to express sincerity and thoughtfulness. They thought before they spoke, and only said what was necessary.

"Starting in the Ming Dynasty it was called Fuxian Lake." Lee dutifully continued. "The miles of soil surrounding all sides of the lake are sand based. But tens of meters deep, there are accumulations of large rocks. These rocks have very structured shapes; there are cubes, pyramids, and also long rectangular slabs. Some were even aligned neatly like sets of stairs or inclines. There was also a stone wall."

Someone asked, "Are these architectural remnants?"

Lee said yes. Some say it was a fallen city, and it looked as such. But as for which city it was, and when and why it had fallen, no one was sure. Currently, experts speculate an earthquake or a landslide. Only underwater archeological research can answer this question.

Ms. Duan and Ms. Lin were awestruck. Ms. Duan even asked, "Is there any written data on the matter?" Obviously she wanted to go and write it up. Xu Yi felt this was a sign of present day professional greed. The older authors laughed it off obligingly, humbly. Only Old Hu acted like he did not hear it, like he knew better.

Xu Yi did not ask anything, and did not act awestruck. Ji Mengbei was pleasantly surprised by this. She was not the type to show off. This was a good thing; why it was a good thing, he was not even sure himself.

Since their hotel was near the lake, every morning Xu Yi would wake up and go directly to the balcony to take some deep breaths and admire the lake view.

In the morning, on the balcony, while combing her hair, she heard the adjacent room's balcony door slide open. It was Little Miss Lin. Then she heard singing: "The white michelia blooms and sends its fragrance ten *li* away; every flower has an enduring love ..." It was a low, soft voice, but not one that sang often. For a moment, the voice was caught, a bit tight.

And then, another voice joined in harmony: "To wear a bouquet you must wear it often; don't throw the bud to the wayside ..." This voice was very clear and intoxicating. It was Ms. Duan.

No wonder they were enjoying themselves. The white michelia tree was two stories tall; the flower branches reached over as the window was opened. But Xu Yi did not recognize the song. Perhaps it was a popular song from their younger days.

Xu Yi checked the schedule. It was not mealtime yet. So she went downstairs. She wanted to wander farther out, but she ended up meandering from one michelia tree to the next, fetching the buds from the branches as she encountered full blooms. The flowers were covered with dew; the color made them look like congealed egg whites. They softened the heart. Upon closer inspection, they looked like the flowers from her childhood—the kind she would buy and clip onto the second button on her coat. But in her memory, the flowers grew on short shrubs. How come they were on tall trees here? She was not so sure they were the same anymore. Why were they called michelias here? What is the name's origin? She thought she must find an opportunity to ask.

Just then, from afar, she spotted Ji Mengbei walking. He was alone, just a silhouette, with the appearance that he did not want anyone to approach him. Xu Yi thought: was something troubling him? If so, what was it? What was it that was so difficult for him to conquer?

In Xu Yi's history, she had never encountered anyone like Ji Mengbei.

Aside from her college professors, classmates, the only men she understood were her current colleagues at the publishing company. Since working there for six years after graduation, the men around her were either too old, or had no opinions of their own. If looks were not there, then there was no interest in hanging out more. She secretly hoped for newcomers who had recently finished college or graduate school, but she had not had much luck. There had not been a single male newcomer in six years.

How old was Ji Mengbei? She did not know his

specific age, but his age seemed just right; it allowed him to glow, to be attractive. Watching him, Xu Yi felt that her life was monotonous, flat, and almost bleak.

She noticed other women had warm feelings towards Ji Mengbei. This couple of days, after getting acquainted, Ms. Lin and Ms. Duan would ask Ji Mengbei to help with their bags; Ms. Lin would give him mineral water to quench his thirst, while Ms. Duan would jokingly say she was jealous.

Ji Mengbei simply coped with it. You could not tell whether he was happy or not happy about it. He neither neglected nor grew close to anyone.

But he never gave a hand to Xu Yi. It seemed it was not intentional; it was because Xu Yi was neither too old nor too young and never needed help, or perhaps Xu Yi just never asked for help in front of him.

In fact, Xu Yi never asked for help in front of anyone. Often times, she walked with her headphones. Not only did she not speak, she also seemed not to hear those around her. The older men were busy letting each other go first, no one paid any mind to taking care of Xu Yi. Chivalry did not span across generations.

Ms. Lin and Ms. Duan only tolerated Xu Yi; they felt this girl was purposely trying to stand out, so they purposely did not talk to her. Nobody bothered Xu Yi, so she decided to hum along with the melody coming out of her headphones. This way, no one could tell who was ignoring whom.

Ji Mengbei seemed to be paying attention to everyone around him, and he was doing so without leaving a trace; how tiring, why bother! Miss Lin handed him a bottle of mineral water; he twisted open the cap, handed it to Old Hu, and then took another bottle from Lee for himself. Ms. Duan was showing some temper, complaining about the difficult hike. So Ji Mengbei said to some of the older authors, "There's probably nothing special to see at the peak. It's high elevation. Don't tire yourselves out. Let's split into two groups. Those who have the energy can keep going; those who don't want to go up can rest and have tea in the pavilion over there." Ms. Duan cheered up immediately, and the elderly also happily agreed.

In the end, only Xu Yi and Lee made it to the top of the mountain. Leaving behind the big shots of the conference, Xu Yi became more active, taking off her headphones, talking and laughing on the hiking trail. Her spirits stirred, her whole countenance brightened. Even Lee took notice.

At the hilltop, they could see layers of green covering everything below. It looked like the entire world was green, and all you had to do was take a step and melt into it. The cool air breezed through their clothes, allowing their pores to breathe freely. Xu Yi spanned her arms wide and yelled, "Ah! Ah! Yoo-hoo-hoo-hoo! Hey!!"

She was carefree in her yelling, as if she was facing a deserted mountain.

Under the shade of the pine trees, the subtle wind blew. Her voice carried the fresh fragrance of pine.

On the last night of the conference, there was the regularly scheduled dinner banquet, followed by a dance.

The dance on the last night was always well attended and popular. For one, the group had spent several days together, so everyone was well acquainted and energy was easily stirred. Secondly, it was the last night, so it was understandable and permissible to let go of inhibitions and show a little enthusiasm.

Thirdly, there was no need to hide what you like or don't like anymore—nothing to be embarrassed about, for tomorrow, each will go his separate way. These are the reasons why the organizers have never had to spend much energy drumming up excitement for the dance. It was always a success. Sometimes they go until dawn.

At dinner time, Old Hu took a look at the fine domestic wines brought over by the waiter and frowned. Lee immediately asked, "If you don't like these, we can ask for other choices." Old Hu asked for a bottle of 12-year-old Chivas Regal brandy. The men at the table joined him in enjoying the brandy, but Old Hu drank the most. He drank until his cheeks grew dark red. He sighed and sighed as he stared forlornly out the window at the lake. Xu Yi thought to herself: at his age, he's still acting like a sorrowful old Werther[1].

Great attention and detail was paid to the dance hall decorations. There were Roman columns and fake ivy vines, floral curtains, and layers of translucent drapery. It was all very sweet and luxurious, but it also

---

1   Refers to the title character in *The Sorrows of Young Werther* by Johann Wolfgang von Goethe.—Trans.

unnaturally separated the room from the woods and the lake outside.

Ji Mengbei arrived at the dance early—not because he liked dances, but because, if he had to come either way, he'd rather walk over on his own accord rather than being dragged by others. Besides, the hosts were extremely gracious; the least he could do was be an abiding guest.

He first asked the two organizers to dance, as thanks for their hospitality over the course of the conference. He then asked Ms. Lin; when he walked her back to the table, Ms. Duan stood up with a happy smile. It was obvious that Ms. Duan danced often. As soon as the music piped up, she was filled with energy; with her back straight and her steps light and smooth, she had the charm of a professional dancer. Ji Mengbei perked up. The two of them glided to the dance floor and made several advanced dance moves. The spectators started to clap. Ms. Lin and Ms. Duan were then swamped by invitations to the dance floor. At this point, Ji Mengbei retreated to the sidelines.

Lee came up and asked, "Why didn't Miss Xu come?"

Ji Mengbei took a sweeping glance across the

dance floor. Even without looking, he knew: of course she did not come. He said, "Maybe she's tired, and resting?"

Lee said, "I checked her room. She's not there."

The light and the sounds, even the smell, from the dance floor were all too overwhelming. It was bearable while he was dancing; but once he stepped off, it was all too much for the senses. After two cigarettes, Ji Mengbei felt numb again.

He quietly exited the room and went outside. The scent of the michelias permeated the air. The moist, cool, fragrant air suddenly washed over his whole body. Walking along the stone path, he slowly arrived at the edge of the lake.

Even before reaching the water, he noticed a silhouette along the water's edge. He thought to himself, "How stubborn." He took another look. The deep blue water and the soft moon made the silhouette look uncommonly thin, like a sheet of translucent fog that could magically disappear in an instant. The image softened his heart.

He walked over, stopping a few paces behind the silhouette's shadow. He let out a gentle cough, hoping not to startle her.

She turned around, her eyes glistening like the water's reflection.

"Why aren't you dancing?"

"Why aren't you dancing?" she asked in return.

"I came outside for some air."

Xu Yi turned away and recomposed her original stance, as if there was nobody else around her. Ji Mengbei looked at the lake, then stole glances at her. This young girl in the night, with her wavering emotions, losing and forgetting herself like a flower blossoming petal by petal in the darkness. This feeling, this scene, seemed to have appeared in his dream once, many years ago. The woman in the dream was not her, but the water was the same, the moon was the same, the shiver up his spine was also the same.

He only heard her say, "This lake, it's so beautiful it brings sadness."

He wanted to say something, but there was a gust of wind. He said instead, "Let's go inside?"

Xu Yi asked, "What did you say?"

"I said, let's go inside."

"No, you wanted to say something before that."

Ji Mengbei replied, "It was nothing, I thought of an old poem."

"What was it?"

"The water flows dreamily, I am melancholy like the king."

Xu Yi stood still. Enchanted, she asked, "Who wrote this poem?"

"Emperor Wu of Liang."

"An emperor? An emperor can write such a poem?"

Ji Mengbei felt a need to change the mood, so he said, "Are you coming in?"

Xu Yi replied, "No, not going in."

Not only did she not want to go inside, she also did not want him to go inside. But he felt he had stayed too long and said too much, so he only said, "Then I'm going back in."

Alone, he stepped back from the water's edge, and walked away without looking back.

Xu Yi never appeared for the rest of the night. Ms. Lin and Ms. Duan were tired from dancing, and asked where Xu Yi was, but Ji Mengbei said he did not know. He thought, a girl must be quite stubborn to sit alone by a lake rather than join the group and have fun. Besides, he already tried to coax her inside, what else was he supposed to do?

Xu Yi continued to sit by the lake, alone; Ji Mengbei never appeared again. In her mind, he was obviously doing this on purpose; in a fit of anger, she sat in the same spot until sunrise. Only then, with her body frigid, did she walk back to her room.

The next day, everyone got ready to depart. Due to different flight schedules, they left for the airport in three separate cars.

Xu Yi was in the second car. When she opened the car door, she saw only Ji Mengbei inside. They were on different flights, but their flights were only 20 minutes apart, so they were assigned to leave together. Alone together in the same car, plus the odd way they ended their encounter last night, all made for an awkward car ride.

The driver was not Lee but another young lad with bright red cheeks. Xu Yi asked, "Where is Lee?" The young lad said Lee left early to send off Old Hu. As he spoke, he handed over a small bamboo basket. "Lee asked me to give you this. He said you like these."

Curious, Xu Yi took the lightweight basket. On the top there was a layer of vibrant green leaves. She swept them aside, and look! Underneath, there was a full basket of michelias! They were all partially bloomed; some were white, some were a pale yellow. It was obvious they were picked from several different trees. It turns out, the touching sentiment that she had been searching for throughout this whole trip was waiting for her right here.

Ji Mengbei said, "So great!" It was not clear whether he was referring to her or to the flowers.

Xu Yi smiled lightly, but did not respond. She thought, maybe it's always like this; pleasant surprises only come when you're not looking. As soon as you looked for them, you will be disappointed. At most, you will not be disappointed, but a pleasant surprise is no longer possible.

Xu Yi layered the leaves neatly back into the basket, then placed the basket on her lap in full seriousness. She looked determined to bring them back home.

At the terminal, the young lad with the red cheeks left, leaving only Xu Yi and Ji Mengbei. After they checked in for their flights, they sat down, with an empty seat between them. Neither said a word. Xu Yi's flight was up first, but her flight was still an hour away. The driver was afraid there would be traffic coming to the airport, so they planned extra time. Now the two have to wait it out together.

Ji Mengbei watched as Xu Yi looked left and right. She appeared determined not to speak first. He secretly sighed. This girl was quite temperamental; luckily he did not pay her much attention the past few days, otherwise she would be even more arrogant. But in the end, he could not act like just another acquaintance, so he said, "It's still early. Let's get something to drink."

Xu Yi replied, "Are you talking to me?"

"Of course I'm talking to you. There's no one else around," Ji Mengbei said with a laugh.

"For many days I have been living like a fish, not using my vocal cords at all. Suddenly someone is talking to me. I have to get used to it." Xu Yi said this, as she wiped the slate clean after last night's encounter.

"Really? That day yelling on the mountain top, weren't you using your vocal cords?" Ji Mengbei sensed her attack, so he retaliated with the same tone of voice.

Knowing that he heard her that day, Xu Yi gave a smile, but quickly withdrew it. But because of that quick smile, the atmosphere between them instantly eased. Ji Mengbei asked again, "Let's go." She stood up and walked with him.

Ji Mengbei ordered a hot tea, but insisted on getting just the hot water. He had brought his own tea leaves. Xu Yi ordered a mango juice. She watched as Ji Mengbei took out his personal stash of tea, dropped a few leaves into the cup, and poured hot water from the glass teapot. He did this all very seriously. She thought, he did all this for a cup of tea, what kind of man is this. Xu Yi was born in Jiangnan. She knew many tea drinkers would settle for less when they traveled.

"Is it good?" Ji Mengbei took a sip of his dragon well tea. He looked at her glass of thick, gooey yellow liquid with pity and suspicion.

Xu Yi said, "It's not fresh squeezed." This type of canned juice is never any good. Xu Yi secretly envied Ji Mengbei's cup of tea; clean and light green, just looking at it quenched her thirst.

After a while, Ji Mengbei asked as if only out of politeness, "Did you have fun?"

"Did you?" Xu Yi punted back.

"I had a lot of fun."

Xu Yi shot him a glance. She thought, then why did you ignore me? But if she mentioned it now, she would just sound childish. Even if he answered, then what?

She thought with sadness about how Ji Mengbei will never know how cruel he was. In the past few days, it was the perfect time, the perfect place; if a good man had come along and treated her well, she would have been so thoroughly happy. These would have become the best, most memorable moments of her life.

From the very beginning of the trip, Ji Mengbei had appeared. It was a hint towards possibilities of a happy ending. But those precious days are now in the past. That hidden possibility never came to fruition.

The season, the weather, the lake, the michelias; they all fulfilled her wish. Only he did not.

Now it's too late.

Xu Yi found Ji Mengbei inexcusable. He never cared for her. These few days, he flattered everyone and made them all happy. Now, he wanted to extend a hand to coax her; what gave him such confidence? He was too idealistic. Xu Yi was determined not to let him have his way.

Ji Mengbei did not know what was on Xu Yi's mind, but an upset woman is always a source of stress for men. The more he wanted to ease the tension, the more upset Xu Yi became; the more upset she became, the more he felt he needed to tread carefully. Watching him speak cautiously just made her more bold. It took Ji Mengbei all his might to come up with something to say, but his ideas all trickled out like droplets rather than a flowing river. It all quickly evaporated like mist in a desolate desert.

So he decided to be silent, firmly silent. If he stayed silent, there was no potential for embarrassment. And since both of them were silent, it became a sort of mutual understanding.

Slowly, their mutual silence became comforting. Both relaxed, their postures softened, their faces lit up, and each gained renewed composure.

From afar, they looked like the most intimate couple—the kind that sit across from each other with only a pot of tea between them, who completely understand each other without ever uttering a sound.

Time did not slow because of the silence. All of a sudden, it was time for Xu Yi to board her flight. Startled, Xu Yi got up to leave. She wanted to bid farewell; but standing there, she did not know what to say.

Ji Mengbei said, "Let me walk with you."

Xu Yi said, "No one is watching. Why should you?"

Ji Mengbei said, "You think I care what other people think? You don't know me."

Xu Yi watched him, and thought to herself, of course I don't know you. How can I? Did I ever get a chance to know you? Did you let me? Her eyes swiped complicated glances across his face.

Ji Mengbei handed her the bamboo basket. "Don't forget this. Carry this wherever you go, and you can smell flowers along the way."

She took it, and continued to stare at him, thinking, racking her brain. He's talking like that again, just like last night, with the poem. It made her think he understood everything, and was open to anything; but in the end, he actually was not willing.

Finally, she realized something. She smiled, but her smile quickly disappeared, and a sudden sadness distorted her face. She turned to quickly walk away.

Ji Mengbei hastily paid the bill, hurried out, only to see her running away, her long hair flowing behind her. Even from her back, he saw sadness. Ji Mengbei was anxious, but he was embarrassed to run after her, so he walked briskly. By the time he caught up, she had already entered the ticket gate.

Ji Mengbei shouted, "Xu Yi." This was the first time he said her name.

She did not turn around. She raised her hand to wipe her face.

Ji Mengbei shouted again. "Xu Yi! Call me!"

She seemed to pause, but she did not turn around. She wiped her face again.

As the plane took off, Ji Mengbei suddenly realized something. He did not have her contact information, and neither did she have his.

So many days, and yet they never even exchanged their name cards.

There was always the assumption that there'd be a chance for them to talk one-on-one, to exchange phone numbers—the number not printed on business cards, the easiest number to contact each other. But when they finally got their time alone, none of their expectations came to pass, only the unexpected disappointment.

Of course, they could ask others for contact information. But to be so clumsy and intentional was not Ji Mengbei's style, and neither was it Xu Yi's style. Therefore, today was their last farewell. She knew this. That was why she cried.

This was not the first disappointment of its kind. There had been many. The most serious one was at his mother's funeral. At the time, he realized he never said a word of gratitude to his mother, nor had he asked his mother if she lived a happy life. He kept wanting to ask her, but he kept thinking it could wait until later. In the end, he will never get a chance to make up for it.

He never knew; by the time he knew, it was too late. He thought they had time to talk. He thought about how he should talk. But in the end, the person he wanted to talk to had disappeared.

His mood suddenly grew heavy. Ji Mengbei thought, what a fool! He was angry with himself.

A wisp of a familiar scent surrounded him, then dispersed. Michelia. This scent could only be described as fragrant. Just like Xu Yi's personality.

It was a present from someone else. She was someone who was supposed to receive gifts of flowers.

She was deserving of this flower. It was Xu Yi and the flowers that brightened this trip. But the person who would send her flowers will never be him. From the outset it was never going to be him. It was doomed. If she understood like he did, then great. But she did not understand, because she is still young.

In the future, how will she remember this trip, how will she remember Ji Mengbei? Will she intentionally forget about this trip?

Sometimes, if people want to forget, they can really forget.

Just now, when the two of them sat across from each other, the scent of michelia flowers permeated their skin and their breaths. It brought calmness. It seemed everything that needed to be said had been said. Their hearts' burden had been lifted. In that state of trance, Ji Mengbei remembered an incident, an incident that he had almost completely forgotten.

Many years ago, there was another woman. He and she met at a writers' conference. He and she were like two halves of a shell; they were extremely similar, extremely compatible. They hit it off amazingly. After they parted, they kept in touch by phone, always with endless things to say.

He did not know she was not single. She never brought up this topic, and he never thought to ask. Sometimes he wanted to ask her on the next phone call; but by the next phone call, there were other things to talk about. There was never a chance to ask such a tedious question. Later, he realized he did not want to ask, did not have the guts to ask, because he felt he could not live without her. At the time, Ji Mengbei was still very young—almost the same age as Xu Yi—and he had very little experience with love. It was therefore easy for him to view the emotions that were happening to him as rare and sacred.

She never mentioned anything about meeting again. But he missed her terribly. One day he could not take it anymore, so he went to the part of the city where she lived. Arriving at the entrance to her building, he felt so anxious that he could not go up. So he ran to the phone booth across the street and dialed her number. She answered. Hearing his voice, her voice brightened like the moon shining through parting clouds. He said, "I'm downstairs." Smiling, she said, "You're joking?" He said, "Look out the window. You should be able to see me." She suddenly went silent, then walked over to the window to look outside. When she came back on the line, her voice had completely changed. She only said four words, but they were four words Ji Mengbei can never forget: "What are you doing?!" Before Ji Mengbei had a chance to react, she hung up the phone.

Later, he was grateful for her. She brought him the most fulfilling passion of his life. And only because of her would there be the Ji Mengbei of today.

Staring at the endless clouds outside the window, he thought, Xu Yi allowed him to remember this past story. He should have told the story to her.

But what would it have explained? Did he want her to forgive him? With Xu Yi, when did he turn into someone who needed to be forgiven?

Ji Mengbei smiled bitterly.

A Miracle Rides In on a Sleigh

S he became depressed when December arrived.

The reason may sound a bit ridiculous: Christmas was coming.

Even she herself did not understand her melancholy right before the arrival of such a festive, joyful holiday. But she really did lose all energy; her face grew pale, and blue-tinted dark circles appeared under her eyes.

Several times, she had woken in the middle of the night. She pulled the curtains open and looked outside, and sighed deeply.

In the past, in her younger years—she is only 33 now; in the eyes of an elder, she is no different than a 23-year-old, but she knew there is a big difference. Her younger years refer to those before she got married—in her younger years, she always had a certain expectation from Christmas.

There were the Christmas wreaths on the shop doors, snowflake patterns, Santa Claus and his sleigh pulled by reindeer in the window displays. There was Santa Claus on the streets, handing out flyers and small gifts. There were Christmas parties and, of course, gifts and party invitations from young suitors.

She was not a romantic girl. She understood that while she had decent looks, in every other way she was an average, unremarkable girl. To live a good life, she had to work hard and make a real effort. "A good life" to her meant this: to have a decent job, to find a good man to marry, and to live an ordinary life. She would be completely satisfied to be a tad above average amongst her friends.

To her, back then, Christmas was a good opportunity to meet her future husband. Every year, she took the festivities seriously, but the holiday itself meant very little to her. She grew up eating rice cakes and drinking soy milk; she never understood the connection between Chinese traditions and Christmas. But of course she never mentioned this to other people. Everyone is having a good time, why spoil the fun?

Living as an ordinary person, she never once hoped for any sort of miracle. An ordinary life was simply a series of ordinary events. Then, a very ordinary thing happened: she married an ordinary guy. He was truly very ordinary; when they began dating, she was afraid she would not recognize him in a crowd. But among all the young men, he was the one who pursued her for the longest time, and with the most sincerity. No one would question her choice, including herself.

She was lucky. Once married, she did not live with her in-laws; she and her husband had their own two-bedroom home. Work-wise, she never went to college, but a family relative who was the assistant principal at a high school offered her a job in the library. The salary was not very high, but it was a stable position. She was never dissatisfied with her job, especially when there was constant news of others being laid off. Later, her husband became a designer at a design institute; the salary was beyond her expectations. Everything was a pleasant surprise.

She diligently decorated their home. She watched as their home became a well-oiled machine; she witnessed as her husband grew from a lean young man into a man with rounded contours and a slight belly. When her husband lamented about his new plumpness, she smiled and replied, "This puts me at ease. This way, girls at the supermarket will leave you alone." Her husband never understood this as a witty remark, and instead would either try to reassure her of his loyalty and faithfulness, or laugh at her jealousy.

They were both good people, with similar views about life. They were truly made for each other. In this type of relationship, days go by quickly. Time flew breezily, so breezily they hardly noticed its footsteps.

She felt this was a good home, a good fate. Warm, peaceful, safe; she could close the door and be comfortable, or go out in public and feel proud—as long as pride was within limits.

She thought she had no interest in occasions like Christmas.

That is, until she watched that movie. Her husband had brought home the VCD. There was no box cover, so she did not even know the name of the film. Her husband watched it while she was knitting on the opposite end of the sofa. She had just come across a new sweater pattern in *Shanghai Fashion* magazine. It was a beige cardigan with maroon and dark blue details. It looked traditional without being old-fashioned. It was sweet and nice, suitable for her petite size. So she bought the yarn and started knitting. Most women her age had no idea how to knit; but she did, plus she enjoyed it. Her mother always said: a woman must know how to cook and how to knit. Even if the world changed and all else failed, as long as a woman knew these two skills, she could do no wrong.

She glanced sporadically at the movie while knitting. Usually, her husband liked to watch action movies. She disliked them, but she always kept him company while doing her knitting. This time, she paid attention because it was a low-key, calm drama. Eventually, she stopped knitting and watched closely, deeply fascinated.

By the end of the movie, she noticed her cheeks were moist. She secretly wiped her face with the back of her hand and glanced over at her husband. He had fallen asleep, a shadow of drool hanging by the corner of his lips. He really had no interest in movies without fight scenes.

She wanted to watch the movie from the beginning, but she had no idea how to work the VCD, so she let it go. She did not know how to work the VCD or the speakers; this is the first time she felt sorry about it. She sniffled and got up to wash the bathtub. She would wait a little while before waking her husband for his bath.

In the story, there is a woman, a westerner—she could never tell the difference between Europeans and Americans. The woman falls in love with a good man, not knowing what he did for a living. Then, for some reason, they split up. They each find someone else, but did not marry, just lived together. Days go by, and they live just fine, but there was always something missing, something neither of them could let go. He and she would wake up in the middle of the night, get out of bed, draw the curtain aside, look out the window, and breathe a deep, long sigh. Once, she had said to him, half jokingly: if they ever miss each other, then on Christmas Eve, they should wait at the top of their favorite church. For several years, the man waited for her, alone in the cold winter's night, while the surrounding crowds celebrated with cheers and laughter. He waited all night. When the sun rises on Christmas morning, he comes back down, in pain and disappointed. In the end, he falls ill. He is in the hospital on Christmas Eve, but he manages to sneak out and painstakingly climbs to the top of the church. He sits and waits at his familiar spot, until he could not sit up anymore, and collapses. Still, he yearns for her, and cries out her name in his heart. Meanwhile, she is exchanging presents with her boyfriend when she hears her old love's affectionate, deeply painful cry. She tells her boyfriend about her past, and confesses that this man from the past is still in her heart, and that was the reason she had rejected his marriage proposals. She takes off, drives to the church, but gets stuck in traffic. She gets out of her car and runs to the church, races up the stairs, and finds him unconscious. She embraces him, calls out his name, and says she finally realizes how much she loved him. He is the only one for her, and she is the only one for him. Finally, he opens his eyes, and says to her, "Since I was a little boy, I have always liked Christmas. Because on Christmas, miracles happen."

She suddenly felt resentful. She had always believed that happiness was like a cup of ice cream. You hold the colorful treat in your hand, and you enjoy it slowly. After seeing this movie, her ice cream image melted into a puddle of sticky liquid. What kind of happiness is that? Did she have someone who loved her deeply, who would be willing to wait for her for years? No. All those years, the men who gave her

Christmas presents were only testing her out, to see whether she might be willing to be their wife. After she married, they all left peacefully without a fight and went about their separate lives. As for her husband, if he did not marry her, he would have found another woman at another time, and would have lived a life not unlike the present.

No one would wake up in the middle of the night and sigh deeply by the window for her. Never.

She herself has never woken up in the middle of the night sighing deeply. She did not want to be that way; it would not be good for her or the man. Her grandmother once said: if your life is simple and peaceful, do not play games or be high maintenance. Games lead to trouble. She believed her grandmother.

Later, she slowly came to realize that some women can afford to be high maintenance, and people would still pursue them. These types of women tend to be very pretty, or very shrewd, or both. She was neither, so these games were not hers to play.

But now, she was losing sleep. She began to wake up in the middle of the night, draw the curtain aside, and stand by the window to sigh deeply. Why the long, deep sighs? Because she had no one to sigh for. She had no one to long for, no one to cause her heartache.

Why was everyone else's love story so much more epic, so much more emotionally dramatic? Why was everyone else's life so much more … full of flavor? She had not experienced much; and yet, at 33, she had already been married for so long. The probability of some sort of miracle happening to her was close to zero.

There was a line from the movie: "A life like this is not called living. It's called surviving." Well said! Why had she not seen the difference between the two before? How could she be considered a woman, not noticing this?

If grandmother were alive, she would definitely accuse her of being a player. If even just thinking these thoughts was considered playing, then she vowed to play at least once in her life. She used to think it was wise not to play games; in fact, it was stupid. It was every woman's birthright to play hard to get, to be high maintenance, to keep men guessing. Once you get older, it is all over.

Perhaps she had someone who was waiting for her? But why could she not recall anyone? There must have been somebody. Thinking harder, she vaguely recalled someone running towards her in the fog of her memory. Where did she lose him? Where is he now? Every Christmas Eve, where was he waiting for her? Maybe he could not take the waiting any longer? She had not forgotten about him. She will definitely meet him. But she could not remember the meeting place. She only knew the time had to be Christmas Eve.

This will be their last Christmas Eve. If he does not see her by Christmas morning, he will give up, or die. And she will lose him forever—lose the only true love that could only happen once in her life.

In this many years of marriage, this was the first time she had a burden of her own. It was not that she did not love her husband. But what did this have to do with her husband? Like the night when she watched the movie and cried. Afterwards, she still went and scrubbed the bathtub and drew him a bath; she even tested the water temperature to make sure he would not scald himself. Only then did she go and wake him. That was her life. Nothing had to change.

Her husband would not suffer any harm. Everything he needed was still by his side, including her. But she knew she was no longer the same. She had been awakened by a new kind of love. This love had nothing to do with cooking and knitting and taking out the trash. She never thought this kind of love would descend upon an ordinary woman like herself. But here it was, shining and brilliant opposite the cooking and the knitting and the taking out of trash, the bleak daily life that was her life. It was shameful. She was tormented by this love. It broke her apart, but at the same time it freed her spirit.

Christmas Eve finally arrived. She saw her husband off to work, but did not go to work herself. She called into work and took the day off.

Today she had an important meeting. She had to make the proper preparations.

First, there was the hair. Where should she go? She should pick a good place, where the hairstylists are well trained. They spend time with the customer to patiently discuss an appropriate hairstyle, unlike those cheap barber shops where they roughly ask, "What do you want?"

It had been a long time since she had visited a hair salon. She recalled Hujiang Salon on Huaihai Road; the stylists did good work. So she hailed a cab.

When she told the driver "Huaihai Road by Maoming Road" she felt proud for sounding like someone who frequently visited the trendy part of town.

When the cab arrived at the address, she got out of the car and was immediately perplexed. Hujiang Salon was no longer there; in its place was Gujin, the lingerie store. She knew about Gujin, but she thought Gujin was next door to Hujiang Salon. Why is Gujin there but not Hujiang Salon? She pondered for a moment, then went inside Gujin to ask the clerk. The clerk told her Hujiang Salon had closed for over a year. Gujin took over the salon's location.

She was disappointed in herself, looking for a shop that no longer existed. Caught off guard, she had no idea how to find another good hair salon, so she wandered aimlessly on the street. She came upon a narrow road and spotted a small hair salon. It looked newly remodeled; it was clean inside, and there were no clients waiting, so she went in. She was greeted by a young man in his 20's; he was handsome, with purple and gold streaks in his hair. Years ago she would've found this scary; right now, she found it interesting and unique.

Three hours later, she walked out of the salon

with shoulder-length, tousled light-brown locks. It was young, trendy, and warm, with a touch of flirtatious that was very natural and unpretentious. This would have been too much for everyday; but for today, it was perfect. She had a date. She was very happy with who she saw in the mirror; but she did not want to be too obvious about it, so she just smiled modestly.

The outfit was next on the agenda. She stepped into a designer retail store. She recognized the designer brand name from a fashion magazine. As soon as she entered, the young sales clerk saw her and rushed over to help. This gave her an extra boost of confidence in her makeover—if she had entered with her usual, lifeless ponytail, store clerks in this type of trendy shops would not be so enthusiastic about assisting her.

She took her time to browse. She selected a pearl colored pullover knit sweater, with a high collar that highlighted her slender neck. She also picked out a black-and-white checkered pea coat that was just long enough to touch the top of her boots. Today, she wore black Italian boots with thin high heels. Her husband had brought them back from a trip to Hong Kong. She never thought she would wear them, but today she was very glad to have worn them. They made her look four inches taller, and they brought a slim, attractive curve to her figure.

As she admired herself in the mirror, the sales clerk walked over and said sincerely, "Oh, it fits you really well!" She calmly replied, "Please cut off all the tags. I'm going to wear this outfit now." She did not even look at the price tag. The clerk said, "Would you like me to put the coat and the sweater you wore into the store into bags?" She sensed the envy in the clerk's eyes as she handed over the credit card. She knew this young woman could not afford the clothes in this store. Until yesterday, she herself had no interest in these clothes. Even if she could afford them, she did not fit the style. But now, everything is different. She had an important date.

Stepping out of the store, she immediately felt the gaze of the passers-by. This beautiful, stylish woman, dressed in an elegant coat, carrying two large shopping bags with the designer's emblem, walking alone on the street. She could get used to this nice feeling.

Everyone must think I have designer clothes in these two bags too, she thought. But inside those bags were only her old clothes. She felt a little embarrassed about this, but also secretly pleased. With these two bags in her hands, she is far, far away from the life of cooking and knitting and taking out the garbage. That was someone else's life. Her cheeks flushed red with excitement.

She was getting hungry. It was already two o'clock in the afternoon. She decided to get some food, but she was dressed too nicely for her usual trips to the food court. Besides, the greasy smells and the smoke would ruin her clothes and her hair. After some thought, she decided to go to Pizza Hut. She ordered a small pizza and a glass of juice. She ate with fork and knife, and was pleased with the fact that she remembered how to properly use a fork and knife. The pizza was very good, and she finished it quickly.

Where was she going next? This question suddenly surfaced.

But the real question was: what was she doing out here today? If she were honest with herself, the answer would be "I don't know." But today, she did not want to play by the usual rules. That would be boring.

She knew.

She was waiting for that one person. An important person, a person she must see today. She did not want a one-time affair and then pretend nothing happened—she was not that kind of woman. She was serious. She was convinced that this meeting could change the lives of two people.

He must be out here. Perhaps he was already waiting for her somewhere. She was sure. She just did not know who he was.

She left Pizza Hut and strolled along the streets for a while. The gazes of the passers-by no longer excited her. She began to worry. The sun had set, and twilight was quickly covering the sky.

She had not expected night to arrive so soon. Whether her love, her miracle would come true tonight remains to be seen. Her throat felt dry. The only other time she felt this sensation was before her college entrance exams. She was too nervous then, and she bombed the test. Afterwards, she lost all confidence to give the college exam another try.

Maybe she needed something to drink, to soothe her throat and to calm her nerves.

Just then, she spotted a coffee shop. She entered,

went up to the second floor, and was happy to find the room mostly empty, including several empty tables by the window. She sat down at one of the empty seats. The waiter brought a glass of water and asked for her coffee order. She looked at the menu, which had pictures of every coffee beverage available. She chose the coffee drink with the prettiest cup in the pictures. Honestly, the only thing she knew about coffee was that she knew nothing about coffee. By picking the pretty cup and saucer, at least she won't be disappointed in that aspect.

The coffee shop was quite spacious. It had an understated western flavor, as if the intention was that its guests would relax in comfort.

Her drink arrived. Thick white foam covered the top of the drink, complete with dots and star designs. She knew she was not supposed to drink with the spoon. As she pondered about how to bring the drink to her lips, she heard a voice call out her name. She knew she must have been mistaken, because it was impossible.

But that voice walked up next to her and said her name again. She looked up and saw a man, a tall stranger standing by the edge of her table. Her first reaction was that he had mistaken her for someone else.

"It's really you!" said the man with a smile.

She stared at him for a few seconds, and then remembered. "It's you!"

He looked at her, up and down, and said, "You've become so beautiful. I almost didn't recognize you."

She was so excited, she wanted to tremble; yet she restrained herself. She returned a smile as a true beauty who was used to receiving compliments. Then she heard herself say, "How are you, Mr. Class President?"

He was the class president from junior high. He was the object of many girl classmates' secret crush, while she was the quiet unknown ugly duckling. But he was always warm and friendly towards her; she figured it was his duty as class president. Later, he was admitted to the city high school, while she could only get into the district high school. The two of them lost contact after that. When he went another city for college, he had sent her a New Year's greeting card. During summer break, he visited her at her home in Shanghai. Her mother even had the nerve to implicitly ask about his family situation, which embarrassed her to no end. Her mother was always so clueless: he was a student from a well-known university, and she was just a nameless clerk; why would he be interested in her? She was not interested in him either; she was a girl who knew her limits, who did not give much thought to the things she knew she could not have. She had few worries, few despairs.

Looking now, he really was quite a handsome man. Had she never noticed before, or had he transformed into this over the years? He was tall, stylish, with thick hair, grace, and a beaming smile. He very naturally sat down across from her, as if he was the person she was waiting for all along. The waiter came to take his order. He looked at her cup, and said, "I'll have what this young lady is having." His voice sounded like velvet.

They began to talk. Their conversation flowed like water, a stream that veered endlessly, eastward and westward. They talked about their old classmates, their lives over the years, their current work, and many, many other things. She learned that he worked for a foreign investment company. As for her work, his comment was, "A library? It fits you. You've always been a quiet person."

She looked down and smiled. All these years, no

one had ever told her what type of personality she had. But to hear it now, from him, was not so bad.

He suddenly said, "Do you know? I used to like you very much."

She was shocked, and asked him when this was. It was during junior high. And because he had this quiet, shy girl in his heart, he never found a girlfriend in college. But when he visited her in Shanghai that summer, she seemed indifferent, plus her mother was acting strange; he figured there was no hope. When he graduated and returned to Shanghai, he found out she was married. "I was distraught for a whole day! Someone stole my favorite girl!"

He said this with a smile, but then noticed her blush.

He was embarrassed, as if he realized she was still the same introverted shy girl from those years. He was afraid that speaking of the matter so lightly might upset her, or she might think he was being casually flirty. So he explained sincerely, "What I say is true."

He was silent. She was silent. She did not want to speak. She only wanted to sit here quietly, across from him, eyes looking down, to feel his presence. When they were in school, whenever he spoke with her, it felt just like this.

She never thought it would be him. Someone had really loved her. He might still love her. In the past, he must have woken up in the middle of the night, gazed out the window, and sighed deeply for her. Her heart filled with sweetness, an overwhelming warmth that was ready to melt.

If she had not loved him before, then she loved him now. He did not realize what he had done for her. On this Christmas Eve, when she had pushed herself to the brink of hope, he rode in like a true knight in shining armor, just in time to rescue her from the depths of sadness and desperation.

His cell phone rang. He apologized and took the call. She still kept her eyes down, still ready to melt at any moment. She thought, "No need to apologize. You can do anything."

However, she heard him speak in an impatient voice, "Stop your nonsense. I'm meeting with a client. It's a he. He's a foreigner." He immediately ended the call.

"Sorry, that was my wife. She's a very nice person, but she thinks too much," he said, his voice no longer like velvet.

"Women are not like men. Accommodate her a little bit, and you'll be fine." This was the standard woman's response whenever a man complains about his wife. But she did not say this out of etiquette. She simply did not want to talk about this anymore.

She was enthralled by his recounting of the past, but she still had a few questions for him.

For example: "You've reached quite a high rank at your company. Why do you still have to come out in public and meet clients? Most people couldn't ask for a better situation."

He did not immediately respond. She looked up at him and noticed a very strange look on his face. He was staring firmly at someone behind her. Suddenly, she felt a chill above her head. The chill spread to her face as she heard a shrill voice shout, "I knew you were seeing another woman!" And then, all sounds quieted as every pair of eyes in the room looked over in their direction.

Tracing the people's gazes, she turned around as water droplets hang off her eyelashes. She saw the woman behind her. The woman was very young. On a normal day this woman might have been a beauty, but at this particular moment she looked like a raging tiger, ready to pounce and pull her to shreds.

It was this tiger who dumped a full glass of water onto her head. Two waiters instinctively responded together; one wiped down the table while the other wiped down her clothes, even saying "I'm sorry" while doing so.

By now, she had woken up. She noticed the waiter was using a rag on her clothes, and quickly pushed his hands away. Knowing everyone was watching, she calmly took out her handkerchief—she disliked paper tissue, and always carried her own handkerchief. She stopped her hands from trembling, and slowly dried her face and her hair. Fortunately, she thought, her hairstyle was a little messy to begin with. It can't be too bad now. Then, she calmly watched him, to see what he would do.

His facial expression turned ugly. She used to read books that describe angry characters whose faces bloat up like pigs. She thought it was an exaggeration, but now she realized there really was such an ugly facial expression. He stood up, brushed his wife's face in a slap, and said, "Are you crazy? Isn't it enough you're crazy at home? You have to come out here and cause a scene?"

"Didn't you say you were meeting a foreign client? A man? I had to come and see this client for myself. Is she a foreigner? A man? Tell me!" That woman looked her up and down, and said, "One look and I can tell she's up to no good, dressed like this to seduce another woman's man. So shameless!"

She was shocked, but it was not anger. It was similar to the shock of the first time she tried *malatang*, the spicy numbing pepper soup. She never thought this drama, which she assumed only happened on television shows, would play out on the stage of her own life. She never thought she could look like a woman who could seduce away a man from his wife.

He was speechless. He grabbed his wife's hand, rushed to the stairs, and then disappeared.

It all happened so quickly. That woman's appearance was like a short-lived illusion.

She sat still, as if to consider whether he would return. People began to look away as a show of their best gesture of kindness towards her. Several of them secretly glanced at her with sympathy and curiosity.

Just then, a foreigner with chestnut hair and blue eyes appeared. He looked left and right, but did not find who he was looking for. He sat down at a table near her, and dialed his cell phone. Then he shook his head in confusion.

She knew who he was. No, she did not know who he was, but she knew who he was looking for. She also knew he won't find him, because that person has already gone mad for the day. It was probably impossible to have a normal conversation with that person today.

She thought about it for a moment. She felt her English was good enough to explain what happened to this man, so she approached the foreigner and asked if he was waiting for so-and-so. Unexpectedly, the foreigner replied in fluent Chinese, "Yes, that's him. He's the person I'm waiting for." She breathed a sigh of relief, and explained that that was her old classmate, that she had run into him here, and that he had to leave for an emergency. If you're not able to reach him now, don't worry, he will definitely get back to you. No, he did not ask me to stay here. I just haven't left. I saw you looking for him, didn't want you to worry, and took the liberty to come over and tell you what happened.

The suspicion on old blue eyes' face disappeared.

Finally, he smiled. "Thank you, I'll have a cup of coffee before I go."

She smiled, and figured it was time to go home. She said goodbye to old blue eyes, who happily said, "Merry Christmas, old classmate!" She had forgotten it was Christmas Eve. How did she forget?

Suddenly she realized they had not paid yet, so she grabbed the rolled-up bill in the small cup on her table and paid by the register near the stairs. She knew he would be upset that she paid, but it did not matter. It really did not matter by now.

Back home, her husband had not returned from work yet. So she cooked dinner. He got home just as dinner was ready.

She had changed out of her new clothes. He had not noticed her new hairstyle. Only after dinner did she mention, "I didn't go to work today."

Her husband only said "Oh" as he waited for her to continue.

"I went shopping, then had my hair done."

He looked up at her. "It looks very nice."

She hesitated for a moment, but continued anyway. "I bumped into an old classmate at a coffee shop. We chatted for a while."

Her husband said "Oh" again. He waited, but she did not say anything more, so he figured nothing special happened, so he did not ask for more details. He started to read the *Xinmin Evening News*. He knew his wife was loyal and honest. There was nothing he needed to worry about.

The next morning, while at work, the front desk called to say there was an express package for her.

She wondered: who would send her an express package? What could it be?

It was a very large, very beautiful box. The wrapping paper had a red background, and was covered with a snowflake pattern, along with reindeer pulling a sleigh. There was also an eye-catching green ribbon. Removing the wrapper, she saw an elegant box. Inside the box was a vintage wide-brimmed wool hat in gray. It seemed to be an excellent match for her new coat.

She looked at the tag. It was a brand she did not recognize. It was not in English, so she let it go. But she knew this: it must be very expensive. Did he really think she was the type of classy, trendy woman who should wear this type of hat? She shook her head and chuckled.

She knew who sent the gift. She paused for a moment, then dialed a number—her husband's. "It's me. I received a gift today. It's from my old classmate. He must've felt bad about me paying for coffee. So he sent me something."

As Santa Claus could bear witness, she was telling the whole truth.

But one thing she was not ready to tell anyone: miracles really do happen on Christmas—miracles beyond your wildest imagination.

Lady Boss

When women approach the age of thirty, age invariable becomes a source of worry. One after another—27, 28, 29—the years fly by like a speeding train, and the last stop is within sight. Of course, it's not the last stop of life, but it is the last stop of the prime time of life. Only after turning 30 do women realize those precautions and worries were unnecessary—a luxury really. When the calamitous event befalls a woman, it's never the disaster like she had anticipated. Thirty-one is one, isn't it? After that comes two, three, four ... it goes on and on. Put together some clothes and makeup, and by age 35 or 36 there is a new level of grace that rivals that of a 20-something. By that time, guessing her age is like guessing the year of a fine wine; only a master can do it.

But in the end, things are not the same. You can fool others, but you cannot fool yourself. Gradually, the ramifications make themselves known. First: no more crying for no reason. At times of sadness, if a woman loses control and lets the tears pour out, her face will swell, and her eyes will bulge out like a gold fish. The lines around the eyes are exposed. Even using ultra-soft, ultra-plush tissue on the nose does not stop it from turning red or peeling. Anyone who takes a glance at this face will know her disappointment and misery. Oh, who could have imagined that even crying is a privilege for the young. Second: no more late nights. A young woman can go a night—even two nights—without sleep, and the next day she can go back to school or work like nothing happened. Her appetite is still strong, her skin still glows, her eyes are alert; not a single yawn as she goes about her day. Now? Without a good night's sleep, by the next morning her skin is pale, and her eyes are dry and lifeless, complete with two large bags underneath. After a couple of nights of sleeplessness, her face becomes gray, and she can only remedy with makeup. Even foundation powder does not cooperate: a thin layer is not enough, but a thick layer makes her face look like a mask.

And this is precisely the mask that Zhong Keming wore to work today. She had just sat down, and was pondering whether she needed a cup of black coffee to revive herself when Han Xiaoyan rushes over like a gust of wind. "Boss, boss, please sign here."

It was the expense report from her business trip to Hong Kong. Zhong Keming signs it, then watches in a daze as Han Xiaoyan walks away. The silhouette of Han Xiaoyan's back says one word: lightness. The lightness is not only because Han Xiaoyan is slender; her body also possesses a certain bounce and flexibility. Zhong Keming is slender as well. But since she is ten years older, her bounce has disappeared. As for Han Xiaoyan's face, there is nothing unique about her features, but her skin is flawless—fair, soft, and young, like the petals of a flower that has absorbed ample water and nutrients. Moreover, this flower is not wilting anytime soon. It is just beginning to bloom—her skin is taut, her features springing upward like energetic dance steps. This face is ready to shine for years. Thinking of her own thick, makeup-laden mask, Zhong Keming could only let out a defeated sigh to herself.

Who wouldn't want to shine naturally? Who doesn't know that looking beautiful without makeup is best? But it all requires certain assets. The first is good genes. The second is youth. Youth, she does not have anymore. As for her genes, they have not been as reliable lately. Perhaps this is why her own husband became infatuated with that other younger woman? Zhong Keming was reluctant to criticize or accuse the girl of being a slut; she was more refined than that. Even privately, she only accused her of being shameless, of having no manners, and that karma will catch up to her in the future. Basically, Zhong Keming is a woman whose words match her heart.

As soon as Han Xiaoyan left Zhong Keming's line of sight, the smile on her face immediately disappears. She goes back to her desk, sits down, then suddenly jumps back up as if something bit her. She stands there, thinks for a few moments, then runs back out again.

Once again, Han Xiaoyan runs into the bathroom. She quickly dodges into one of the stalls, pulls her pants down, and sits down. She flushes for no reason. She takes a deep breath, then looks down into her panties. Her heart sinks. Nothing. The red she was expecting is nowhere to be seen. The moistness she had felt earlier made her excited and surprised; it sent her heart racing. But it was all a false alarm.

According to her regular calendar, her period should have started two weeks ago. But so far there is nothing. She blames Sha Lequn, who refused to use a condom that day. Han Xiaoyan relented, thinking she could take emergency contraception the next day. But the next day she received an unexpected assignment to go to Hong Kong. In her excitement and the rush, she completely forgot to buy the pills. Only when she returned from her trip did she remember, but by then it was too late to take the pill. She was shocked, but was hopeful that luck was on her side: it was only once, what are the chances? However, her period never came. Disaster.

Of course, she is not going to let her boyfriend Sha Lequn off the hook. First she hit him repeatedly, then she cried for two hours. Sha Lequn was nervous at first, not being sure how to comfort her. He then suggested going to see a doctor with her. This was not what Han Xiaoyan wanted to hear. She had hoped for her boyfriend to come up with some ideas: if she is pregnant, what would they do? At first she had never felt that she must marry him. But at this point, he should say: "It's not a big deal. If you're pregnant, then let's get married." They have been together for two years already. He should give her the benefit of this option. Besides, is this not his fault all along— first, not using a condom; second, not reminding her to take her pills. Even if he did not intend to harm her, he may as well have. She has always had a heart of confidence, but now that confidence is gone, and she is relying on him to provide a safety net.

But Sha Lequn is still acting like an idiot. He says, "Do you feel pregnant?"

"How would I know what pregnant feels like? I've never been pregnant before!"

"Then let's go check and find out!"

"You make it all sound so easy! If I am pregnant, then what do we do? You take it so lightly, because you're not the one going through this!"

"Lightly or not, we have to find out the facts first, don't you think?" He is like a fly, circling around then landing back on the same candy wrapper.

"We find out, then what? Here, I'll just tell you, I'm pregnant!"

Sha Lequn freezes. "There's always a way."

"It's all you!"

"You can't blame me for everything. Women should manage these types of things, just like we men should always take care of paying the bill."

"What did you say? How can you compare this to paying the bill? Here, I'll pay the bill and you get pregnant out of wedlock! Yours is money, this is ..."

Han Xiaoyan cannot say clearly what this is. Actually, Han Xiaoyan knows that there is no need to go to a hospital. They can easily go to the pharmacy and pick up a home pregnancy test. They can find out in a few minutes, with 99% accuracy. But how is that any different from going to the hospital? Aside from running into an acquaintance at the hospital, isn't everything else the same? Not knowing—if she is pregnant—how she will live, or how she will die; or that no one will come to comfort or share the burden, and that ultimately she has to face the verdict alone! Furthermore, she knows that this verdict is for two people, but the accomplice could very well run away unpunished, leaving her doomed. Even if she escapes to the edge of the world, the verdict will follow her wherever she goes—because the verdict lives inside of her.

Of course, if she does not want it, they do not have to get married. In today's world that is not a fresh idea. But why must she be the one to make this decision, to commit this sin? She has also heard having an abortion on the first pregnancy can result in certain gynecological conditions, as well as psychological impact, all of which are unpredictable at this time.

For the first time in her 26 years, Han Xiaoyan realizes men and women can never be equal. The joy of loving can be shared by two people, but the consequences are all for the woman to bear. Troubles immediately reduce a woman from a princess to a commoner; if she starts out as a commoner, then she is condemned to hell. The man can say a few words and watch from the sidelines. If he decides to bear responsibility, he is celebrated as a great man, because he has proven his mercy, his sense of responsibility, and his courage—he essentially becomes a saint. But in reality, whether she decides to abort or to raise a child, isn't it all a disaster? Why must she endure the disaster, and yet be grateful for the person who caused it in the first place? How outrageous!

She does not want to let him have it so easy. If she is pregnant and takes the decision lightly to have an abortion, then she will never know Sha Lequn's intentions. She wants him to clearly state his commitment or his refusal before bearing her burden. In other words, she will not bear this burden until she gets to the bottom of his true intentions.

Every day, Sha Lequn urges her to go see a doctor, but she keeps delaying, hoping his worries would pressure him into revealing his intentions. But her tactic has not gotten her the result she wanted, though they remain on good terms. Every day, every hour, her mood worsens. Oh Sha Lequn, who knew you were such a heartless wolf in sheep's clothing. Actually, even if you want the baby, I may not necessarily want to have it. Even if I consider marriage, I may not want to marry you; and even if I marry you, I may not want to be a mom yet. She feels this is a sort of required lesson for all women. If he asks to marry her, she can consider killing two birds with one stone. If he doesn't think twice about asking her to have an abortion, then she has no real choice but to break up with him. Having the child will be out of the question. However, he keeps being vague and indecisive, making no move and keeping his thoughts to himself. This makes her anxious to no end. I'm taking you on! Sooner or later, you'll have to say something.

But there is a price to playing this game, and that is using her body as a chess piece. There are moments of discouragement. But she is already in the game, and she cannot retreat so easily. If she compromises, how will she spend the rest of her days?

Every night before she falls asleep, she secretly prays. She prays to God, then Buddha, hoping that she is not pregnant, and that her period would start the next day. In exchange, she is willing to give up the battle and not pursue Sha Lequn's intentions. They can go back to being a couple that muddles along.

If it were not for her distracted state of mind, Han Xiaoyan would have already noticed something different about Zhong Keming. She is like a young fox, laying in wait in the meadows with her ears perked up, sensitive to every change in the wind and of her surroundings. She knows to make requests on days when Zhong Keming's clothes reveal her sunny mood. She knows to disappear when Zhong Keming has had a bad meeting with management. When she hears that Tao Cong go for business trips, she automatically works overtime and even orders takeout for her. She can even accurately estimate her menstrual cycle; unlike her male colleagues, she would never bother

Zhong Keming with minor troubles on the days when she has wenstrual cramps. It's not to say that Zhong Keming is the kind of woman who deliberately acts emotional, but sometimes her hormones would go up and down like a rollercoaster. But Han Xiaoyan gets it. Someone famous once said, "Compassion comes from understanding." Han Xiaoyan feels this makes a lot of sense; she understands everything about Zhong Keming, so she can secretly sympathize. Meanwhile, Zhong Keming perceives this understanding from her subordinate as respect and compatibility. She needs this, and therefore she sees Han Xiaoyan as a stable, reliable girl who is easy to get along with. For several years, these two women of different ages have managed to get along without incident. Their coworkers find this incredible.

But this time, Han Xiaoyan's radar on Zhong Keming is malfunctioning. It's no wonder, since she is mired in her own fear and frustrations. How can she be expected to operate at her normal sensitivities? The entire office now knows about Tao Cong's affair; she is the last one left in the dark.

The story is quite absurd. Tao Cong got involved with a female colleague who is many years younger. Tao Cong is forty this year; the girl is maybe twenty-four, twenty-five. The most incredible part of the story is this: the girl is not pretty at all. And the part that everyone is longingly waiting for—to see conclusive evidence of—is that Zhong Keming knows about the affair. Now, they will watch how she plans to have mercy on him, or rather how she would endure this humiliation. Everyone thinks Tao Cong is an idiot. Zhong Keming is absolutely beautiful. She graduated from a prestigious university, and became one of the few female members on the management team at her current company. She earns an impressive salary, wears nice clothes, drives a nice car; she is smart and decisive, never flirtatious, and superbly well-mannered. As for child rearing, she has done well beyond reproach as well. She gave birth to a child at a normal age. She is a woman who takes good care of herself; by looking at her, you can never tell she has a five-year-old daughter already. A woman like her can be considered a role model in the city's white-collar ranks. If she did not despise those thick fashion magazines so much, she could have had her impressive career published and her face on the covers multiple times. So, to have a wife like this, and still have an affair to the point where his wife finds out—Tao Cong must have lost his mind. But for some reason, everyone still goes about their business and their merry way. Is this a case of schadenfreude? No, this is just a human instinct to rationalize and make sense of it all. Why must Zhong Keming be so fierce all the time? When she widens her big eyes, her opponent feels instantly shorter. When she gets upset, it's a hurricane; whoever dares to speak is guaranteed to be silenced by the storm.

Even a woman like this has her weakness: her love life. The more illustrious her life, the less she can afford to lose. The unknown can fall and slowly pick herself up; the notable has to be caught with her face in the mud under the watchful eyes of spectators. People chime in as if cheering: "Oh, that was a hard fall!" "How could this happen?" Then they open their eyes wide to watch how she wipes off her bloody wounds and pick up her disheveled self.

Basically, Zhong Keming stays calm and collected. This is her only choice; to put it another way, this is her choice out of having no choice. Other than her makeup being heavier than usual, there is no sign that she is experiencing any sort of trauma. As soon as she arrives at the office, she forces herself to forget everything happening at home. If she brings her private life into the office, her work could easily suffer, and her husband's affair would eventually topple over her life and her career like dominoes. She wants to limit the extent of the disaster to one aspect of her life. Her husband is no longer dependable; she cannot afford to lose her dominance and future at the workplace. She can do this, on her own wisdom and her own willpower. This is how she encourages herself.

She notices that the majority of her colleagues have retracted their prying attention from her. She has closed her door shut, without letting a single ray of light through. They have given up. I'll let it go this time! If you pry into my business again with ill intentions, you will all have to pay! Zhong Keming thinks this with a sneer.

But once, when she returned to the office, from outside the door she could hear a room full of laughter. The laughter was like a warm tide washing over. She could pick out each familiar voice. What was making everyone so happy? Infected by the laughter, she quickened her step and walked in, hoping to dive into the sea of laughter. At that moment, she almost forgot about Tao Cong and the disaster he had brought upon them. But when she appeared in front of everyone—no, when her face was seen by the first subordinate, that person immediately stopped laughing and looked as if he was slapped in the face. He not only stopped laughing; within one second he had wiped any traces of a smile completely off his face. The others followed his lead; seeing or realizing that Zhong Keming had appeared, they all responded. Some froze mid-laugh, and walked back to their desks with that frozen half smile. Others were even more embarrassing, and slapped their forehead pretending to have forgotten something before running away. They all scattered like mice avoiding a cat. A few seconds ago, here was a fresh meadow and wild flowers and a spring breeze. Now, Zhong Keming was facing an empty wasteland.

Zhong Keming had just built herself back up, but now she falls flat all over again. She understands her subordinates; she knows they were not joking about her or even talking about her. This is not because they were particularly kind to her; it is because they have no unity or trust amongst themselves. Even though individually they were watching her life drama unfold, together they did not trust each other enough to discuss the matter openly. Just now they were sharing a joke that had nothing to do with her. The question is, why do they all act like they had seen a ghost as soon as Zhong Keming appears? Because they know that Zhong Keming is the most miserable, most unfortunate, most unspeakably bitter woman under the sun. This kind of woman cannot bear to see a smile, just like you would not laugh at a joke in front of someone who just had a death in the family. To do so would just mean you are tone deaf or your mother never taught you any manners. All of her coworkers are well educated, and so of course they would never do such a thing.

For the first time, Zhong Keming understands her situation. She has become someone in front of whom others cannot even have fun or tell a joke. It's no use forcing herself to put up a strong front. Even having to put up a front is part of her "pathetic" state. It's true: her husband doesn't love her anymore, she has no idea how to face that fact; how can she be expected to seriously manage this emotionally bulletproof bunch? She who is deemed the most principled; now how can she face them?

The next morning, Zhong Keming made up her mind to go to work late. In more than ten years, she'd always been the type of person to show up on time in the morning and work until late into the night. Even when she had her daughter, she took only one month off, foregoing the enjoyment of three more months of maternity leave. Her daughter lived with her husband's parents; Zhong Keming visits once a week over the weekend to see her daughter. Getting to work on time was her unshakeable habit. But now, it does not seem to matter. Tao Cong has not come home. He has hidden out for several days; because as soon as he appears, Zhong Keming would pick up the nearest object, whatever it was, and throw it at him. It might be a pillow, it might be a cup, or it might be a platter full of vegetables.

Being alone is quiet. Tomorrow she can sleep in late. The sky may fall for all she cares. A woman can make a decision like this when the sky has already fallen.

But the next morning, at seven thirty, Zhong Keming wakes up on time as usual. She gets up reluctantly, and moves deliberately slow in washing and putting on makeup. Seeing that it was still only a quarter past eight, she eats the croissant that had been sitting there for who knows how many days. She reads yesterday's paper, then looks at the clock again: 8:45. If she goes to work now, she would still be on time and arrive at her office by 9:30. Such a wretched life! She utters harshly in her heart, then unlocks the door and heads out.

Even as she drives, she was reluctant. Why go to work? Why suffer the stares and walk through that narrow empty space? In fact, if she does not appear for a half day or a full day, no one would say anything. She does not have to explain herself to anyone. It's just that she has never done that before. Zhong Keming suddenly realizes the real question facing her: at this moment, 9 a.m., other than the home where she does not want to be, and the office where she does not want to go, where else can she go? She had never considered this question before. Facing it now, she feels a bit helpless.

Suddenly, a nearby movie poster catches her attention. The picture was a bit messy, but the movie title was very clear: *King Kong*. She has no interest— she has no interest in movies, or *King Kong*, or whatever other title. But she suddenly sees a way out. She can go see a movie. She cannot remember how many years it has been since she last saw a movie. It might have been when she and Tao Cong were still dating. Now, she can go watch a movie, in a place where no one would be watching her, in a space where she can quietly spend some time. She thinks of a cinema near her apartment; she can go see a matinee, it can be any movie. Afterwards she can show up at the office as if nothing happened. She does not have to make up any excuse about traffic or other causes of delay.

Once there, she sees the first showing is at 10 a.m., so she buys a ticket, then heads downstairs to the coffee shop to buy a latte. She finds a seat near the window to watch the street scenery. She notices the people on the street all had no smiles on their faces. They are all rushing somewhere, most with furrowed eyebrows; some even clench their teeth as if in pain. Some have a look of contempt, target unknown. This makes her feel a bit better. At least she is not the only one overwhelmed and at a loss.

As ten o'clock approaches, she goes upstairs, enters the theatre as directed by the ticket agent, and finds herself alone in the whole theatre. She is a little surprised, but realizing what time it is, she is relieved, and even feels a little wicked pleasure towards those who are working. The door shuts and blocks out all the noise from the outside. The lights dim to just the right darkness for hiding. She puts her jacket on the next seat, puts her head on the seat back, and lets out a comfortable sigh. Such a good feeling for only twenty yuan—why didn't she think of this before? She pays no attention to the movie title or the plot, and instead falls into a deep, satisfying sleep. When she hears footsteps and opens her eyes, the theatre attendant is already opening the door for her to exit. She stands up and puts on her jacket when her eyes catch a glimpse of someone else in the theatre. Obviously that person entered after she did, and the movie had an audience of two. She takes a quick glance and sees it's a woman who must have been engrossed in the plot, since she has her head down and is wiping tears from her eyes. She finds it amusing, and was about to redirect her glance when that woman raises her head. Zhong Keming simply cannot believe her eyes: that person is Han Xiaoyan.

Han Xiaoyan sees Zhong Keming too. A pair of

sleepy eyes meets a pair of teary eyes; they both widen. They are very much not supposed to meet. Actually, this is the time when they are very much supposed to meet, but the place is not supposed to be here, with faces they were not supposed to show.

In addition to both being embarrassed, Han Xiaoyan has the additional panic from being caught not at work during work hours by her boss. This is absolutely abysmal. If she were not in such a foul mood, she would never venture out to the movies during work hours. Who knew a workaholic like Zhong Keming would be in the mood for the movies too?

In the end, Zhong Keming is ten years older and quickly calms down. In a lazy melancholy voice, she says, "Never thought I'd be here, right? Keep it a secret." Han Xiaoyan smiles—one of relief and gratefulness. Zhong Keming sees this bright smile on a face that had just been crying, and feels a sense of authority. In her satisfaction she remembers to be kind. "Did you drive? If not, I'll give you a ride."

For the rest of the day, Zhong Keming realizes: recently, Han Xiaoyan has been acting strangely. This little girl has not been prying or gossiping with the rest of them, but she is making slow progress with work. She has been hastily finishing projects at the last minute. Is she fighting with her boyfriend? Even her clothes seem off: baggy jacket with jeans, and layers that don't match. She has never seen her so distracted. Now, she is sneaking out again. For two days she has been frequently leaving her seat; is it smoke breaks or cell phone breaks? She is certainly not going to the bathroom; no one would go to the bathroom in such high frequency.

Six o'clock, time to go home. Zhong Keming sees that Han Xiaoyan still has not left. If she is working overtime as usual, she always comes by to discuss dinner takeout. But today, she just stays at her desk, as if thinking or in a trance. The office is empty. Zhong Keming walks over, stands behind her, and lets out a gentle cough. Han Xiaoyan jerks her head around with a startled look.

Zhong Keming says, "Why haven't you left?"

"I have nowhere to go. And I don't want to go home. I'm so bored."

Zhong Keming ponders for a moment, and utters something she had never asked any of her subordinates before: "Why don't we go out for dinner together?"

They each pick up their things, then walk one after the other to the elevator. Arriving at the basement garage level, Zhong Keming says, "Let's take your car." She is tired, and does not want to drive. They both get into Han Xiaoyan's old Santana. Zhong Keming mentions a place, then closes her eyes to rest. Arriving, Han Xiaoyan sees it is a Vietnamese restaurant. The restaurant is decorated in a mix of Southeast Asia and French styles. It appears strong and bold, full of sophistication and luxury. The first time Zhong Keming came was to meet a client. At the time, she felt she had entered a scene in a movie; it felt too romantic and not suitable for a woman like herself. Today, for some unknown reason, she blurts out this place. Perhaps she needs to prove a point, or wants to splurge to console herself.

Zhong Keming hands the menu to Han Xiaoyan. "My treat. You choose." Han Xiaoyan does not hesitate, and orders cane sugar shrimp, a curry beef, mixed vegetables, and a Vietnamese appetizer platter. If she's not paying there is no need to be polite. Finally she says to the waiter, "Plus a young coconut." She asks for her own beverage, and lets Zhong Keming order her own. Zhong Keming says, "They have very good well drinks. Their cocktails are not bad either. Sure you don't want one?" Han Xiaoyan shakes her head; not sure if she doesn't drink, or if she is not in the mood to drink. Zhong Keming chooses a red wine from the drinks menu. "Bring this first." When the food arrives, it all tastes good. Han Xiaoyan eats seriously, without saying a word. When she is almost done, Zhong Keming speaks up: "Missy, is there something on your mind lately?"

Han Xiaoyan is surprised slightly, then lets out a sigh. Zhong Keming says, "A fight with the boyfriend?" Han Xiaoyan says, "No fight, can't work up a fight. Someone like him, I can't even have a satisfying fight with him."

"Men these days, they're really a little disappointing. It's maddening to try and be serious with them."

Han Xiaoyan says, "It won't affect my work."

Zhong Keming says, "What are you talking about. I know you don't need to be reminded of that. I can't care about you unless it's about work? For so many years, I've always thought of you as a little sister."

Han Xiaoyan is an only child. She has no big

sister, and there has been no shortage of men willing to be like a brother to her. But this is the first time she has heard the words "little sister" from another woman. Her heart is warmed for a moment, and she utters "thank you" before looking down to drink from her coconut. Remembering the acceptance and kindness she showed at the movie theatre, Han Xiaoyan feels that what she says is sincere.

Zhong Keming lets out a sigh too. "Actually, your age is better. There are no troubles. You have youth as a cushion. At my age, I cannot afford to lose."

Han Xiaoyan feels she cannot stay silent any longer. Hastily, she says, "I envy your status. You have a career, a family; your child is growing older, and yet you are still so young and beautiful. If I can be like you, then I'll really have no worries."

Smiling, Zhong Keming watches her for a few moments. She looks sincere, and doesn't seem to be hiding; she really does not know about Tao Cong. Secretly breathing a sigh of relief, she leans back on the chair. At least one person doesn't know yet. At least one person still thinks of her as a successful, happy woman. Zhong Keming realizes she had never needed someone else's approval to stand up tall. For this couple of days, she finally can relax. But why does she want to cry as soon as she relaxes? I must not cry. I must not cry. Whatever happens, I cannot cry in front of colleagues and subordinates. But, in front of whom can I cry? These days, in front of parents, in-laws, and her daughter, she has been swallowing her tears. Now, just cast a small stone, or even a speck of sand, and a flood of tears would burst forth.

"Why don't I have worries? I'm worried to death. If I could go back to your age, then I'd be fine. I would make many different choices. I might not have married Tao Cong; I might not have had a child, leaving myself vulnerable to others."

Han Xiaoyan smiles, and suddenly comes out with this: "Sister Keming, is there a suitor chasing you, is that what's bothering you?"

Zhong Keming scolds, "Nonsense! You say this just to make us old women happy. Didn't your mother teach you to respect your elders?" Her tone of voice relaxes the mood of the conversation.

"Then what are you worried about? In our eyes, you are simply an earthly immortal saint!"

"Immortal saint? Well, god knows!"

"I'm serious. How does a woman know when to

get married and when to have children? How did you decide in the beginning?"

Zhong Keming had been pondering this same question more than once the past several days. "In the beginning, what did I know in the beginning? If I meet a nice man who is good to me, I'll marry him. When I got pregnant, I had children. I did not know what these things of life mean. Once I understood it all, everything had already happened. In youth, there was no fear."

"But maybe you just can't think too much about these things. Whether right or wrong, do it while young. Like right now for us. We can think all we want but still have no answer. Time has been spent thinking. If it's not managed then there's no getting married."

Speaking so frankly, their conversation has become intimate like that between confidantes. This is usually something to be avoided between colleagues, between supervisor and subordinates. Zhong Keming and Han Xiaoyan are well aware and abide by this point. But now, they just want to trample on this habit. Both of them, heavy hearted, have a strong need to be with someone they're not supposed to be with, to shout together, to laugh together, to cry their eyes out together. Turns out the solid gold that is self-control, wrought by perseverance in the workplace, has now turned into mush. The two of them quickly reveal the original female trait of being guided by emotions rather than rational sense. Those unshakeable principles end up being weak and powerless. At first, those principles would pop up as reminders; gradually, however, their volume grows fainter until they eventually shut up and walk away defeated.

Zhong Keming flicks her empty glass with her fingernails and says, "It's good, you should have some." This time she orders a bottle then waves the waiter away. She pours two full glasses, and takes a few sips first herself. Han Xiaoyan also picks up her glass and drinks half the glass, then says, "This way of drinking is barbarous. When people see two women drinking like this, it must scare them to death."

"Let them scare themselves to death. Scaring them to death is better than suffocating ourselves!" After Zhong Keming says this, she laughs to herself. Han Xiaoyan also follows in laughter. They laugh as if they took some wrong medication. They laugh until they cannot stop, until tears roll down their faces, until they cannot catch their breath and have to hold their belly.

Their laughter set the mood, and the two of them begin to concentrate on drinking. They cling their glasses and finish the whole glass, then pour another and cling their glasses again. Gradually their bodies relax and everything turns foggy. From their perspective, there was no one unlovable; there was nothing they couldn't laugh at. They could not tell whether their faces were starting to flush, or if their vision was starting to blur. There is not enough wine. Again! One more bottle!

"What do you want to do the most right now?" Zhong Keming asks with a smile while sprawled on the table.

"I want to find a most handsome prince, and marry him," Han Xiaoyan says.

"Then you and he will have a child. It has to be a son, to inherit the throne. The royal family does not welcome girls. Of course, first you have a son, and then you have a daughter. You can even have a pile of girls."

"I don't want them. I'm scared. I'm scared." Han

Xiaoyan covers her ears and begins to shake her head violently.

"What's to be scared about? Children are a lot of fun. You must breastfeed them yourself, raise them yourself. Otherwise, they won't be close to you when they grow up. Then all your efforts will have been wasted."

"I don't want my efforts to be wasted. I don't want to put forth an effort. I don't want to be a mother." Han Xiaoyan has not put down the hands from her ears, but she can still hear.

"Then do you want to be a woman at all? When you have one in your tummy, then you're done for, no way out."

"I can get him out, crumple him, toss him in the toilet and flush. Then there will be nothing."

"You will experience so much pain—first, physical pain; then, heartache. It will kill you, the pain will kill you."

Han Xiaoyan says in a tearful voice, "What can I do? What can I do? Sister Keming, I'm going to die, what can I do?"

Zhong Keming suddenly grows silent, then lifts her head from the glass and shouts at Han Xiaoyan,

"Are you pregnant?"

Han Xiaoyan feels like a knife had slayed her. She exclaims and begins to cry. Zhong Keming quiets down and seems to have awakened. Her face becomes serious. Han Xiaoyan lifts her head to look at Zhong Keming, only to see her face had changed from rosy red to pale white. Zhong Keming hisses out, "No wonder."

Han Xiaoyan stares with puzzlement from her fuzzy, teary eyes. Zhong Keming's eyes begin to wander like countless thin, sharp knives. "I knew it. Why would he be interested in you? Even if you're young, he wouldn't become infatuated and lose himself like this. You were calculating him all along. Did you do it on purpose? Is the child really his? Did you tell him he's your first man, and this is your first pregnancy? He must've relented, and wants to take responsibility, is that right?"

Han Xiaoyan shakes her head. "He did not say he would take responsibility. Besides, I don't want the baby either—not now. But I cannot bear to kill him. I don't know whether I should have him, whether I should find him a father. No, it's not my decision; he's the one who can't decide whether he wants to marry me. I don't know. I don't know anything anymore."

"You still say you don't know? You already have him reeling, and you still say you don't know? You don't love him, do you?"

"Don't love him? I don't know. It doesn't matter."

"What are you saying? If you don't love him why are you leading him on? Release him!"

"But what about the child? If I don't keep the father then I can't keep this child. If I don't keep the baby, then I don't need to keep the father. If I keep the child, some day I'll eventually find a father. If I keep the father, then we can have a child in the future. What is this all about?" Han Xiaoyan tilts her head and cannot figure out her own problem.

Then, Zhong Keming's cell phone chimes. She looks and sees Tao Cong's message, asking to meet with her for a good talk tomorrow. She tosses the cell phone aside, and says to Han Xiaoyan, "For a good talk. Talk about what? Tell me, will you break up or what?"

Han Xiaoyan says innocently, "He wants to break up with me? He hasn't said that."

"If he doesn't say it, does it mean you can't say

it?" Zhong Keming reaches over and grabs the front of Han Xiaoyan's shirt. She attempts to pull her clear across the table, but she has no strength to do so, and gives up half way. She shakes her randomly, as if wanting to shake her into pieces. "You tell him! Tell him! Break up, break up immediately!"

"Fine, I'll break up then! Men like this are no good anyway. He can't even say a simple thing. I have no respect for him!" Han Xiaoyan seems encouraged to take a new direction.

"Then it's a deal? You break up with him, and I'll ask for a divorce and tell him to get lost! Someone like him deserves this ending."

"You? Divorce? When did you marry him?"

"What are you talking about? We've been married for eight years. Don't pretend you didn't know!"

"Impossible! He once said that women like you are tough to marry. He'd rather die than marry you."

"You shameless vixen!" Even Zhong Keming herself did not anticipate the effect this comment has on her. As soon as Han Xiaoyan's words reach her ears, she lays a heavy-handed slap on Han Xiaoyan's cheek.

Han Xiaoyan holds her numb face and speaks in slurred speech. "I didn't say anything wrong. Why would Sha Lequn marry you?"

"Sha Lequn ... what? I'm talking about Tao Cong, Tao Cong! That heartless man who has dog food for a conscience, who breaks my heart, and who shames my name. What am I supposed to do from now on?"

Han Xiaoyan's face begins to burn in pain; actually it has already swelled up. The pain wakes her up, and she begins to speak coherently. "You don't know what to do from now on, but why start with slapping me?"

That night, both of them do not recall how they got home. But worse, they both remember everything that was said and done that night—everything the other person said, everything she herself said. They remember everything.

Two women who are too close to each other, who know each other's unknowable secret, are like a sizzling smoke bomb, ready to explode and tear both of them to pieces.

Zhong Keming was just considering countermeasures when suddenly they were not necessary anymore. One week later, Han Xiaoyan resigned. She even said she had not found the next job, and just wants to go home and rest. Zhong Keming sneered in her heart: she must be getting ready to have her baby.

She will never know—she does not need to know—that Han Xiaoyan was never pregnant. Her unusual physical pattern was just a result of stress. Han Xiaoyan had finally worked up the courage to go see a doctor, and the pregnancy test result was negative. That night, the relentless red tide comes flooding back, and she had nowhere to run. Sha Lequn very carefully took care of her, as if she was actually pregnant. Afterwards, Sha Lequn brought up the topic of marriage for the first time. Han Xiaoyan just smiled, and gave no answer.

As for Zhong Keming, she gathered the strength to take a pre-emptive strike, and initiated a divorce with Tao Cong. But Tao Cong disagreed. He said that girl is already out of the picture; he wanted to put their family back together again. He even made the move of asking his parents and her parents to intercede. Zhong Keming was not moved. Finally, Tao Cong brought out their daughter. Seeing their five-year-old, Zhong Keming's heart softened, and she retreated. They eventually went back to the way they were. Heart restored, her work flourished again. Sometimes, when her eyes fall upon the empty desk that was Han Xiaoyan's, her face would feel a slight twitch.

Before she dies, she can send for Han Xiaoyan, and invite her to return a slap to her face, Zhong Keming thought.

But before that day, there is absolutely no desire to see her again.

Listen to the Night

When the phone rang, I was not expecting anything.

"Hello?" I said, weakly.

"... It's you! How are you?" a strange man's voice suddenly struck my eardrums.

"You are ...?"

"You wouldn't know the name even if I said it. Last time, on a rainy night, I had called." He seemed to be suppressing a chuckle. Must be a prank call.

"You have the wrong number." I was ready to hang up.

"Not the wrong number. I'm looking for you. You've forgotten, but last time we chatted for a long time. That's right, you said the cherry blossom in your garden was about to bloom. They've all wilted by now!" he said hastily.

These words were like an invisible hand that pushed open the door at the dark end of a corridor. The light rays shone in, revealing the silhouette.

It's him. Even though he was still a stranger, he

was "that" stranger, not someone else.

"How do you know my phone number?"

"I don't know."

"Then how did you call here? Last time you said you randomly dialed a number."

"This time, my finger was sleepwalking. It randomly dialed these digits. I did not expect to hear your voice. This is great." Behind his voice I noticed a smile, like the sun shining behind thin overcast clouds.

About a month ago, perhaps more, when I was still wearing a thick sweater, I had heard his voice. That day I was leaning on the sofa, with a blanket on my lap, torturing the TV with the remote control. My parents were already asleep. Finally, I could be outright idle, without their pity and without their questioning eyes pricking me in the back.

Channel one: commercial. Channel two: also a commercial. Channel three: melodrama. The heroine was shouting hysterically in clumsy Mandarin. Channel four: opera. The chubby Madame Butterfly batted her eyebrows as she belted out several harsh high notes. Channel six: "There is a link between England and June," Simon Templar said while drinking champagne on the grass. "When you enter into complete solitude, you feel heaven." Roger Moore looked the same after all these years; with his perfectly combed hair and an almost fake smile, he is beautiful as a cream cake.

Then, the phone rang. It was so late, who can it be?

"Hello?"

"May I chat with you?"

"... May I ask who this is? Who are you looking for?"

"You don't know me, and I don't know you. It's raining outside, and I want to chat with a stranger."

At the time, my first reaction was: there is something wrong with this person. But his tone was calm and his voice soft and clear, unlike someone mad or drunk. I looked out the window; I could see the wet, shimmering road in the distance. Indeed, it was raining. I grew a tinge of trust towards this stranger. It's like they always say: "Don't talk to strangers." But in fact, strangers are the most trustworthy.

"How did you get this number?"

"I don't know. I randomly dialed it. I had dialed two other ones. One was an old man who was hard of hearing. The other was a man; I didn't like his voice, so I hung up."

"You want to chat with a woman?" The sad youth of today are no longer looking for love on the streets; it's hard to imagine they would try their luck randomly on the phone.

"I want to chat with someone with a nice voice, preferably a woman. A man would work too."

I stayed silent for a bit. I'm not sure why I did not just hang up. On a night like this, having someone to chat with on the phone was more appealing than fighting with the television channels. Furthermore, if it bothered me I can end the conversation at any time. I don't even have to worry about being polite; all I have to do is put down the receiver softly. Let's chat!

"What are you doing?" I asked.

"Watching TV. No, not watching, it's just on. I went out to the terrace, realized it was raining, and suddenly really wanted to chat with someone."

"No friends?"

"Someone I could call up at any time? No. My friends, I have to be in an especially good mood before I would go look for them."

"It seems you're not in a good mood?"

"It's been not good." There was a sigh. Was he smoking or was he sighing?

"Why?"

"No particular reason. What is there to be in a good mood about? If there is nothing, then there is no good mood. I feel that to not be in a good mood is normal. Good mood is happenstance, a breakthrough."

Meaningful. I feel the same. I said, "Hold on." I moved the phone to the sofa. I laid myself down, leaned the pillow on the arm of the sofa, and picked up the receiver again.

I do not remember how long we talked or what exactly we talked about. It was as if it all happened in a dream. He might have told me that his room looked out to a cluster of buildings, and it was pitch dark. At night, after the rain, it appeared solemn. He said he lived on the 13th floor, an unlucky number. I forget everything I might have said. If he had not called back and mentioned the cherry blossoms, I might have believed that I had just fallen asleep on the sofa that night, and that the phone call from the stranger was all a dream.

On that rainy night, I had talked about the

cherry blossoms. I thought I had forgotten about the cherry blossoms outside my window. But then to mention them to a stranger on the phone! I might not be so hopeless after all.

I feel a bit of gratitude towards that stranger. This time around, at the end of our talk, I said, "Remember my number. Save your finger some trouble next time it sleepwalks." I believed him; he really did not "remember" my number. He went back and forth a bit, then said good night.

The strange thing is, my heart was not bothered one bit. Usually, I do not take the initiative to give out my number, and especially not to someone of the opposite sex. Even this is a bit disingenuous, as if I were some innocent cute young girl. In reality, I am pale and weak, not a bit attractive, and not young at all.

On top of that, it has been a while since anyone called.

I shut myself in the room and did not change out of my pajamas all day. The blinds were closed tightly like my heart, refusing the rays of light.

There was a wine glass in front of me—long stem,

tulip shaped. There was some residual wine left inside; it had already become half crusted like rust stains. In my arms was a small melamine waste bin; inside, there was an egg roll bag, half-sliced peach kernels, and pine nut shells. There were also some old dried plums that have turned amber, and a bunch of napkins.

My appetite is amazing. I can eat a large pile of junk food in a day. If I have a stomachache, I go to the bathroom and vomit it all back up. I would probe my index finger into my throat to induce vomiting. I have had lots of practice.

The waste bin that is always with me is a new year's gift to myself. On the night before Chinese New Year's Eve, I took the store voucher, went to the designated store, and saw it in the household department. It was very lightweight, with an automatic lid that shuts close after something is thrown inside. I bought it. Jing once said, you always like to buy containers; cups, plates, tins, all of it. He also said these containers always help me hold good fortune. Today, if he saw that my new year's gift to myself was a waste bin, what would he say?

What kind of good fortune is that? Now, I wish I could stuff myself into the waste bin.

Today is the weekend. My weekends are invariably spent with junk food and the TV. Even though there is no joy, at least it saves energy. Since the incident, I no longer expect anything or fight for anything. I just want to save the trouble; if I can sit then I wouldn't stand, if I can lie down then I wouldn't sit.

I absolutely despise the sun and all bright lights. I cannot stand the feeling of being defenselessly exposed to broad daylight. I don't want any ray of light to get a glimpse of my wretchedness.

I have no friends. Any kind of friendship, in the face of continued indifference, would lose its moisture, wither, and dry up. I don't like their "I understand everything" attitude. What do they know? They don't know anything, and yet they ceaselessly encourage me to be strong, be normal. In fact, they just want me to be heartless like them. I hate their disturbance. I successfully refused all their concerns and help, and left myself in the desert of time.

Occasionally, I would want someone to bother me, perhaps even to raise a quarrel. But that does not happen. That "finger sleepwalk" stranger, what is he doing now? My intuition tells me he is not a frivolous person, nor is he old and depressed. He also has some sad grief, searching for someone to listen—someone who would not hurt him.

It is a dangerous thing to expose one's wounds. One must be certain it will not be subjected to rough treatment. Sometimes, even being scared and stunned can shatter open the wounds. Unmeasured laments and sympathy are like recklessly touching an old wound with a leather-gloved hand.

I told the stranger my phone number, but he did not call. I was a bit disappointed, but immediately thought, "Was I putting my hopes on a stranger? In this world, who can count on hope?"

Even Jing cannot.

Jing is the most cheerful man among all the men I have met. No, he is an anomaly among men. He has lush thick hair, rosy cheeks, straight and white teeth; when he smiles it's like an uncontrollable flood. His body has a refreshing fragrance, but it is not like any cologne. It made me willing to lean on him and close my eyes amidst that magical air. Sometimes I secretly opened my eyes to see him, only to meet his eyes. Suddenly embarrassed, I would escape a few paces away from him.

Jing is constantly full of energy, full of light.

But after knowing him, I began to cry a lot. Reading novels, quarrels with him, or if he glances at another girl; or even just bad weather would cause a burst of tears. Jing called me "rain child." Whenever I cried he would say, "Today's weather forecast is completely off. It's raining again!" Even I thought it was strange. There is nothing to cry about; why do my tears drop at any small sourness of the heart? But I could not hold it, I could not control any of it.

Perhaps I had a secret sense that knew the future that awaited us, and cried to prepay for a sadness that would be difficult to pay in one lump sum?

When Jing left, I had not one tear. When I rushed to his bedside, he was already in a coma. I waited by his side day after day, and was barely hanging by a thread. So when the doctor said, "OK, no need to rescue anymore," I was silent, and suddenly fell down next to his bedside and lost consciousness. The chord string I tightly held on finally snapped. It had since been dangling within my body, occasionally drifting, but all without making a sound.

Within the year after Jing died, I did not talk to my parents. I hated them. Had it not been for them, I would have left with Jing; why stay in this cold, dull world? I know Jing is not the only man in the world. I also know I can start over; dream, love, and raise children. But I have no way to act on it. I have no strength. When Jing was alive, we did not say we would spend a lifetime together. Perhaps I was not thinking I would marry him and only him, but after he died I felt I could not live on. Someone so close, so close; someone so healthy and positive; how could he just disappear? I thought he would be by my side forever, but now he is missing from every corner of this world. His smile, his eyebrows, his finger, his voice, his breath; how many times have I traced them with my fingertips, felt them with my eyes closed. It is all gone, as if it never existed. Even his promise, it is as if I heard it in a dream.

What am I supposed to believe? Such an absurd life, such an unreasonable fate. Jing is like a shooting star, brightly crossing the path of my life. Only after his light is gone do I realize this whole world is deserted.

The stranger called on another rainy night.

"I think you must still be young, at least younger than me," he said.

Did he say "young?" I laughed.

"It is not polite to inquire a lady about her age."

"Sorry. I just can't help but want to know if it's the same as I imagined." He laughed. "But, it really does not matter. To not know is just as well."

"You probably want to chat with a pretty lady? Let me tell you, I am not." There is nothing to be embarrassed about. I can talk straight to the point.

"You are very candid, and sensitive. People like you make the man by your side nervous," he said.

"You are not the man by my side." As soon as I said it, I was slightly shocked. This sharp talk, did I just say it?

"Do I have a chance?" he pretended to say in a frivolous tone.

"Don't sound so old and depressed."

"What are you doing now?"

"Eating. I have nurtured a habit of reading while snacking since childhood."

"What are you reading?"

"A book by someone who just committed suicide. You won't know it." It is a young author who jumped to his death. This is a book of his essays. His friends spent money to have it published.

"Look down on us science types. To be honest,

I also like history and literature. But when I took the university exams, only the bad students wanted to study liberal arts, so I chose science. In retrospect I really got on the pirate ship."

"Liberal arts people also say they got on the pirate ship. Everyone is like that. Everyone else's load is easy; the next mountain always looks higher than your own."

Oh, college! It all happened before God created the heavens and the earth.

I got distracted, and the person on the phone asked, "What?"

"Nothing. It has been many years. Where have the days gone?" I sighed.

"Yeah. Sometimes thinking of the past is scary. Thinking of the time still to come is even scarier."

Why did he feel the same way? My mind thought one thing, but my mouth said, "Still so young, why so glum? Should have fearless high morale."

"Do you have fearless high morale? Don't scare people," he quipped.

I grew quiet. I didn't want to sound too serious. But I couldn't relax either.

"Do you have a special story? Maybe through

deeper conversation, I feel you have one." Out of my silence he popped this question.

The burning pain from a star flashed across my heart. But, he didn't know anything; it was just something to say. He was only a stranger.

"And you? Do you have one?" I asked back.

"Nothing too special. My father died when I was seven, my mother remarried, I grew up in my uncle's home. I had a childhood sweetheart girlfriend. We broke up a year ago."

"Why?"

"She was pregnant, and the child wasn't mine."

"So you didn't want her?"

"Unless she didn't want that child. But she insisted on having it." I could not tell if it was anger or pain in his voice, like he was telling someone else's story.

"Then what?"

"She gave birth. Now she is having a tough time raising the child alone. The child's father did not marry her." His voice stayed steady, but ended with a tinge of sadness.

"You feel it was unfair to you? Or you feel bad for her?"

"I feel bad for her. I can't stand to watch, but I am in no position to help her. I cannot act too cowardly, do you agree? She wronged me, we don't have a relationship anymore, wouldn't you say?"

No. Otherwise it would not still bother you. You want to help her, perhaps you want her to regret things, and perhaps you still love her. You would not admit it now. I said, "I don't say. Of course, if you cannot digest it and try to force yourselves together, you will both grow tired."

"Thank you."

"Thanks for what?"

"For not making a big deal."

He did not ask me much else. I guessed I could tell him, someday in the future.

Turns out, other than death, lovers can have such a cruel ending. Oh heavens, don't you know we humans have such weaknesses? Why test us like this? Can we beg for mercy and bow out of the exam room?

Tears seep into my hair. I have not cried like this in a long time.

This night I slept very well, no dreams.

At the end of the summer, I traveled for work.

That's right. The place I enter and exit during the day is a lifestyle newspaper. This time I had to report on an overseas, large-scale interior design exhibition. The editor-in-chief asked me to visit the southern city.

I was very reluctant. But the team that usually traveled: one never came back from a business trip, one just got married, and one was sick. The editor-in-chief was in a panic, but still approached me with a negotiating tone: "Not sure if you can put off what you are handling at the moment? If not I will think of another way." I typically do not travel, and the chief never pushed me. I knew this time he was really running out of options. Looking at the snow-like white hair on his head, I could not help but nodded.

Having to mingle with people—a lot of people— is truly cumbersome. I don't like these types of games one bit. But as long as a person is alive, she must deal with things she doesn't like. Besides, my old editor had to deal with me all these years; I should repay the debt.

I chose several sets of wrinkle-free clothes, a book for bedtime reading, a bottle of sunscreen; this is all the equipment for traveling. Before I left, I wanted to say farewell to that person on the phone. But he had not called, and I did not have his phone number.

The southern city really is different from Shanghai. The sky is clear blue, the flowers and trees fill the city with intense brilliance, and the sun shines loud and clear. The street where I stayed was filled with the fragrance of barbecued sausage. As you naturally salivate, you grow nostalgic about life.

The exhibition hall was situated in a captivating venue by the waterfront. Inside, there were models of "homes," as if each were a story box, earnestly waiting for its actors. I felt a little emotional, but it quickly passed. I was working. Where did the melancholy come from? I have always been very clear to separate work time from personal time. I don't even let my moods mix between the two. I interviewed, took photos, recorded and wrote stories, then faxed it all back. I mailed the photos express back to the office. In a few days, our readers will see numerous fabulous photos and descriptions full of warmth. They must think we all love life.

Upon returning home, I saw my parents but did not have much to say. I took a shower, and had a bowl of lily mung bean soup, which is mom's summer repertoire. I invariably do not sleep well when I travel.

Everyday I shake hundreds of hands and bring a big pile of business cards back to the room; it all leaves me mentally exhausted. Now that I have returned to my own bed, I could not help but fall into a hazy sleep.

The phone rang. My mother picked up, then shouted, "It's for you."

I picked up the phone, my eyes still half closed, "Hello?"

"It's me." It is that stranger. "I called many times but could not find you. Your mother asked me who I was calling for, and I said 'your daughter.' She asked who I was, I said 'your daughter's classmate.' She must think I'm strange."

I laughed. He did not know my name. "I was traveling. I don't know your number. I had wanted to let you know."

"Do you want my phone number?" he said. I looked at the area code. It's far away from here.

I said something about the things I saw. "Traveling is not bad. I have not traveled for many years."

"I so miss the roasted goose from that region! So juicy, so fragrant, and crispy. Ah! I must stop talking about it, or else I can't sleep," he sighed like a glutton.

"They sell it here too."

"No, it's a totally different thing. I have to try the authentic one at least once. I must see if our company has opportunities to travel south."

"What kind of company?" Like we knew each other very well. I did not feel weird asking him this.

"Computer company," he said.

A figure wearing a dark suit and carrying a large briefcase flashed before my eyes.

No. Don't piece together a complete picture in the head. Once it's complete, the only fate waiting must inevitably be broken pieces. Let it be a reality of bits and pieces. Even though it is shapeless and in pieces, there is no need to verify the picture, no need to worry. I do not want to know who he is. Just his voice—with real strength behind that faint melancholy, like the sun behind light clouds—a voice that visits occasionally, I do not ask for anything more.

If he knew how important he was to me, would he be scared? Of course I won't let him know.

Chatting with him on the phone became a part of everyday life. Sometimes I felt we were like two people addicted to medicine, each inhaling the same drug from one end of the phone.

In his voice, I gradually relaxed—the same kind where you are with an old friend and you can say anything or not say anything. I often got distracted, as his voice brought up old memories. The voice of a stranger seemed to offer a layer of protection, and the past no longer seemed so untouchable. It became easier to think of the past, and to clearly separate the dreams from the pain. This is great.

"When we met, he had another girlfriend. That woman saw that Jing and I were close, and came to look for me. She was something." I said as I recalled.

"What did you say?" He was always quick to keep up with the plot.

"I said, between us there is nothing to discuss. At this point it's one man, two women; clearly the decision is in his hands. Let him decide."

"Brilliant. Were you certain at the time?"

"No. Two days later, Jing came to find me. He said, 'If you hadn't said that to her, I would still be uncertain of your intentions.' Then we were official." Before my eyes appeared those bright, penetrating eyes; those beautiful, quivering lips. After the first

time he kissed me, I looked at him that closely for the
first time.

Both ends of the phone were silent. He asked,
"How are you? Crying?"

"Perhaps I should not have been with him. I
always wondered, if I had not won him over, maybe
he would still be alive." I finally broke down.

"Nonsense! There are many misfortunes under
the sun. If you took it all upon yourself, how do you
live? Loving you was his own decision. I believe even
at his death he did not regret it."

"How do you know?"

"I know, because I'm a man too. Men don't like
to be forced; even if something goes wrong, we rarely
regret it."

Is that right? I have regrets. I regret that, when
our love was on fire, I did not give myself to him.
We should belong to each other completely, sacrifice
to each other vigorously, and let the most deep and
fulfilling moment of our love last into eternity. This
way, I would have retained a part of him. In our
separate worlds we would still remember all of each
other, rather than traces that grow fainter and less
tangible. If I had known he would leave so suddenly, I

would not have restrained myself at his hinting.

After Jing died, I met a man in a bar. He was very handsome. We left together after three martinis. We went to bed together. He was experienced and gentle. When he found out I was a virgin, he was surprised: "Miss, are you angry with your boyfriend?" I cried. I was angry, but not with my boyfriend.

I wept and lamented in a stranger's bed, to mourn Jing, to mourn the unfortunate me, and to mourn everything that should have been ours. We came from an unknown world into this one. The probability of our meeting was small, and our love was miraculous. But we were too late to belong to each other before he returned to that unknown world. I was still young, and my skin still smooth. But what did it all matter if Jing is dead? I was angry at death. Before death degrades me, I would degrade myself.

Now, "in front of" this familiar stranger, I thought of all the precious time wasted. My heart felt like a yellow leaf in the wind.

"Good. Cry it out. Haven't cried like this in a while?" The voice on the phone was warm and clear. Suddenly, I thought I smelled Jing.

"You won't think I am not normal?" I finally

asked. In fact I ask myself often.

"Why would I think that? It is very normal. Your feelings, your current situation, are all very normal. To encounter these events, no one can handle it all neat and tidy. To love someone is to take a risk. He died and you don't know how to live on. Perhaps if he didn't die, he would've loved someone else? Even have a kid with someone else? You would still be hurting." Was he talking about me, or about himself? Perhaps both.

That night, after we hung up, I noticed my arm holding the phone was stiff from shoulder to fingertips. How long did we talk?

I'm not sure why, I know we are in the same age group. He seems to know that I know. One time he even said something like "Those of us born in the 60's." I even guessed he was a year younger, but I didn't ask, because it is not a concern. I gave him a name: "Sleep." He was quick to retaliate and gave me the name "Dream." This way at least we can finally call each other by name, instead of just "you" and "you."

With names that sound like terms of endearment, we seemed to grow closer like old classmates from many years ago, an old neighbor. At any time we could say things like, "You were just five years old with a peach head haircut, how funny!"

Conversations are always late at night. The surroundings have quieted down. All the activities of the day sink down low, while that of the night gradually float up. Hearing, which had grown dull from the tortures of the day, is slowly revived. The eardrum sensitively accepts each subtle impact, through the cheek, into the throat and chest. I sometimes feel his voice is a kind of liquid that I slowly swallow. As the night deepens, with the table lamp as the only sheet of light, it feels like floating on silent desolate water. Two people secluded from the world, in intimate conversation side by side. When we talk, it's like time passing through the heavens and the earth; we do not know when we started, and we do not know when we ended.

Our conversation is like a leaf, a boat without an oar. When the wind blows, the boat drifts gently, slowly, without direction, without destination. If we encounter any obstacles, such as a water lotus or stems of reed, we give it a soft push and the boat changes direction immediately, again without destination.

Sometimes it drifts away and then drifts back. Sometimes it drifts away farther and farther, and we forget our departure point.

At first I thought he had an average sensitivity. He heard my voice and immediately said, "You have a cold."

"Yes, I got it. I haven't had a cold like this in years. My nose is completely stuffed. My throat is killing me."

"Then talk less. I talk, you listen," he said.

I laughed. "Good. If you ask me anything, I can just say 'Yes' or 'No.'"

I did not say much. After a while he felt a bit awkward and suddenly said, "How about I come see you?"

"What?" I yelled.

"You're sick. I'll come visit you, is that so surprising? Can't accept?"

It should not be surprising, but I simply could not accept. I thought for a moment, and said, "If you come it's troublesome for me. I have to get up, get dressed, comb my hair."

"You don't have to do anything. We're close," he said.

"On the phone we're close, but it's not the same in person. I also don't like to see people when I'm sick." In my heart I added: not to mention you're a man.

It is really strange. Two people who are uninhibited and carefree on the phone realize they are strangers once they consider meeting in person. I do not like Sleep's suggestion. He reminded me of this point.

Sleep was quiet for a moment. He seemed to have sighed, then said, "Really, you do not have to ... I know how you look now. You do not look unkempt and you are not scantily clad. You ... are you wearing a night robe?"

I was taken aback. It was already autumn; half the women across the city are probably wearing their night robes. It is not difficult to guess.

"It's velvet," he said.

The wine glass in my hand shook, and a drop of wine dripped onto my robe. It is velvet, the color of the wine in my glass. I quickly absorbed it with a tissue. "How did you know?" I looked towards the window, in that moment suspecting that he was watching me with binoculars from a nearby balcony.

"I had a feeling you were wearing this type of clothing. The color, I can't be sure. It's dark."

"Are you human or a wizard? Otherwise, you have a special power!" I marveled.

"Come on, it's not always like that. Usually I cannot feel anything. But since you are sick, I can sense a bit. Perhaps it's easier to enter your 'space.'" This person, he has something strange about him; but he is accustomed to it and it does not matter to him. This gives him a wonderful aura that is dazzling.

"What are you drinking?" he asked.

"Wine."

"Drink often?"

"Every night. Do you know what kind I drink?" I quizzed him.

"How much every day?" he said, avoiding my question.

"Sometimes half a bottle, sometimes a bottle." When I said this, I caught myself. When did I become a drunkard?

"In that case, I often talk with a person who is drinking. That's good, wine brings out the truth; you won't lie to me." He laughed.

When did I become a drunkard? Probably

the six months after Jing died. I feel I have already calmed down. Past the ecstasy of adolescence, one quickly realizes: agony and ecstasy are the same— they do not last. Those intense feelings are enemies of life. If it weren't for the sudden death, life is bound to suppress it.

I am alive. I am no longer in pain; or to put it another way, my pain is no longer a fresh stroke of bloodstain. It has dissipated and fainted, and has become the background of my days. But, in the end, I lost Jing and everything associated with him. The enormous void that is brought on by this loss cannot be ignored. Empty living, empty feeling, empty dreams—empty, empty, empty. If I choose death, it is not due to sentimentalism, it is because I have lost all interest in this thing called "living." However, since I did not die, I did not have a reason to die later. I then survived day by day without shame. The world is crowded; it should be left to those who love it. For someone like me to still occupy a space in it, I cannot apologize enough to the whole world. Wine is a good thing; it can blur the line between day and night, the boundary between dreaming and waking, life and death. In a wine glass there is laughter from the past. Half drunk and half dreaming, someone's scent surrounds me; if I close my eyes, I can feel someone familiar next to me—as long as I do not reach out to touch him, to catch him.

"You've had too much. It's not good, not ladylike," Sleep actually criticized.

"Are you such a gentleman? I'd be surprised if you don't drink."

"I've had the kind of wine you're having. But I don't want to drink it—it's too moody, too feminine. It's got good mouth feel." He actually knew what I was drinking. I knew it.

"It seems the trend is to add Sprite to it. It's called something Pink Lady. I can't tell if it's using wine to promote soda, or using soda to promote wine. I have no idea who thought of this." Another irrelevant thought.

"I refuse to try it. You better not try it either. It's an absolute atrocity, lose-lose."

In this small way he and I are quite alike: reserved towards new things; resolute at refusals.

"Any nearby?" I thought suddenly and asked.

"What?"

"This kind of wine."

"Yes. What? You haven't had enough?"

I smiled. Even he has moments of cluelessness. "No. Let's make a toast."

"Good idea. Wait while I go get it."

I vaguely heard the sound of opening cabinets, the "pop" of the cork, then the sound of the bottle hitting softly against the rim of the glass, crisp and clear. "OK. You say, what are we toasting to?"

"Hmm ... For tomorrow."

"For our tomorrow."

"For our individual tomorrows," I corrected.

"Good. Cheers," he said, then it was the sound of liquid passing between lips, throat. I also finished the glass in my hand.

"Fantastic. Let's have another?" His voice was irresistible. I actually nodded and forgot to answer. I noticed no one was refilling my glass; only then did I remember it was only his voice that was a few feet from me. I poured myself some wine into the glass, and twirled it slowly by the lamp.

"So beautiful!"

"Truly beautiful," he echoed.

"What color is yours? A little brown, a little purple; bright red upon closer look, with an underlying flesh tone. But those colors are not transparent. This color is transparent."

"Color cannot describe it, but it can describe the color. This color is called wine. A couple of days ago I bought a silk blouse in this same color."

Men who wear this color, especially silk, are typically very handsome and very smart, with a kind of melancholy. "This might be the trendy color for menswear this year. I saw an ad: 'Wine color intoxicates the new mankind.'"

"Really? Fashionable by accident, really," he smiled, self-deprecatingly or maybe disdainfully.

Suddenly I very much wanted to know his clothing, but I do not possess his x-ray vision, so I could only ask, "What are you wearing now? Sorry, you don't have to answer."

"Me? Cotton pajamas, white, with stripes. The stripes are gray, green and brown. My old girlfriend said it looked like a prison uniform."

I like these kinds of pajamas. I like the material. I can imagine leaning on this kind of shoulder, feeling the texture, thickness and warmth with my face. If a tear were to drop, it would quietly and deeply absorb it, leaving behind reassurance.

"They are comfortable," I mumbled.

"We've had enough, your speech is slurred. Go to bed. You still have a cold," he said.

"OK, Mr. Sleep!"

"Good night, Miss Dream!"

"I was near your place today," Sleep said.

"By which street?"

"Isn't there a station by the park main entrance? Behind the station ramp there are several residential buildings. That's where you live."

I did not confirm nor deny. I was used to his strange power. "Where did you go afterwards?"

"I went to the coffee shop around the corner."

I know that coffee shop. It's a crude place, a place for lovers to rendezvous. I thought, if we ever open a love hotel, we would destroy this type of coffee shops. Inside, the lights are dim, and the one-sided benches make it impossible for two people to sit opposite each other; they have to sit side by side. The smell can be bad; Sleep wouldn't like that place. "How long did you stay? Ten minutes?"

"One minute. I took a look around and left without drinking a single sip of coffee. It's been many years since I've entered such a bad place."

"Didn't want to reminisce? Wasn't your first date with your first girlfriend in a coffee house? In the early 80's, where could you go?" I was not sure why I was gloating on his misfortunes.

"You won't believe me, but my first date with her was backstage at her performance. She was still in high school then, and she was on the dance team. Several boys were chasing her hard, but she let me pick her up backstage after the performance. I think it's because we were neighbors. Everyone had left. She slowly removed her makeup, changed her clothes; I sat and waited. I remember sitting on a blackboard on its side, waiting. Finally she came out and smiled at me. I don't know why I felt uncomfortable. When I stood up, she suddenly gave me a kiss. After her kiss, her face flushed red. I could only put on a nonchalant look, but my heart was racing."

"How old were you? So innocent."

"I was in college, so 20," he said softly. I could not hear any sighs.

"Was it her?" I referred to the single mother.

"Yes," Sleep said solemnly.

"Still haven't figured out what to do? Have you

seen her recently?" I couldn't help but ask.

"I don't know. Must I figure out what to do with her? What does it have to do with me anymore? Sometimes when I visit my uncle, I bump into her. The neighbors still talk about it."

She must be very beautiful. Dancers have a refined elegance even if they are not natural born beauties. But they also give off an air of fragility. With an illegitimate child, her days are chilling to think about.

"Is she getting by?" I didn't dare to think about the negative. I turned it around and thought about the practicalities.

"She found a job, and lives with her parents. Shouldn't be any big problems. The problem is, when her child starts going to school, there will be a lot of trouble without a father. Also, what is her plan? Would she spend the rest of her life like this? She's only 27! To see her like his, without anyone to help, I ... Sometimes I feel I am too cold. Not a man. But how can I help her? Why should I? Someone give me a reason!" Sleep tried to light a cigarette. He flicked his lighter a few times; it didn't light, and he tossed it aside.

"At first, why did she ..." I tried to be careful, but still asked.

Sleep smiled bitterly. "You can ask me, but who am I supposed to ask? At first I tried to force it out of her, I even hit her. She would not say. She just repeated, 'you would have to kill me. Stop asking me.' What kind of talk is that? She was my girlfriend, the woman I wanted to marry. To see her like this now, everyone pities her, saying such a good girl, ruined. It's hard to listen to it all, you women are most afraid of this kind of talk. But I'm also ruined, and no one pities me! She knows who ruined her life, but I don't even know who ruined my life. Sometimes, damn it I want to ..."

"Hey! Hey! Hold it. Don't talk like that; your talk can lead to action. If you don't verbalize your thoughts, it'll go away. Once you verbalize it, there's trouble."

Sleep was silent. He picked up his lighter again, and lit his cigarette. He drew one puff after another.

"OK. Don't be upset. I don't understand your girlfriend, but I understand women more than you do. I can think of one possibility, do you want to hear it?"

"Yes. But don't try to console me."

"I would guess she loved you all along. What happened, it was an accident to her too. There was nothing she could do."

Sleep did not respond. I felt him calm down. I leaned on the sofa. I relaxed my whole body and let an unknown force take me into the heart of a stranger of the same sex. This game is not easy. It's not truth telling. It is to take the mess of a narrative from Sleep, take one thread, straighten it out, and follow its lead. Add to it my personal emotional experiences and those of others I witness. I slowly weave a web and use it to soothe Sleep's broken heart.

"It is temptation. Other than the very ugly ones, women face a lifetime of irresistible temptation. Maybe she met a man during a time when you were not by her side, or a time when you were neglecting her. Possibly a middle-aged man, someone completely different from you, is very attractive. The place they met, the way they met, might have been very unique. Girls find that romantic. And that man grew an interest in her at first glance. She knew she shouldn't, couldn't; but it happened so fast there was no way to think about it. Have you read *Twenty-Four Hours in the Life of a Woman*? It's a novel by Zweig. In life, there are moments like this where you don't recognize yourself. We involuntarily jump down what we know are epic cliffs. After the jump, the rest is up to the heavens. Nothing is up to us."

"She didn't think of me? We were about to get married!"

"No. She couldn't think straight at that time. She didn't even think of herself, how could she think of you? In fact, she betrayed herself."

"I always thought she was a very traditional girl."

Wrong. Girls like that have lonely hearts. She feels not ready to resign; she wants to change the "right and proper" scenery, to betray herself a little, and to find something else. The "right and proper" that Sleep mentioned is part of her "self" that she needed to betray. Sleep truly was wronged; he suffered unavoidable hurt, but the hurt was not targeted at him. In the process of a woman's growth, aside from the price she has to pay, there are men destined to pay the price of her breakthroughs.

I thought I should speak a little more plain and simple. Sleep's mind is already a mess. "She wanted to rebel. When someone has been living according to everyone else's expectations, it can be boring; it makes you want to drive off the rails. You two were too good of a fit, things were going too smoothly; ideally you would continue that way. The average girl would have been satisfied. But for an exceptional girl, to end the emotional adventure and to live a simple life is absolutely not her dream."

"Women are so strange. They always want security and stability; but once they have it, they grow restless."

I did not answer, because now is not the time to tell him: in a woman's life, she needs to feel both security and the feeling of helplessly tumbling in love; they just happen to appear in different stages of her life. I continued: "After she got pregnant, she was suddenly brought back to reality. That man couldn't marry her; she also didn't think of marrying him. There isn't much to it. But there was a mishap: she got pregnant. The second mishap was she was too softhearted and could not bear to take the small child's life. If she took care of it secretly, she could have hid it from you; for a lot of women this is easy. She could not. For a person to face this situation alone, coupled with the pressure, she mustered up all her strength to rebound. She made a decision to take her mistakes to the end, regardless of everything else. She did not explain and did not ask for forgiveness. This actually was not her decision; she had no choice."

At this, I heard a faint sob. The profile of a stranger, girl, weeping, faintly passed before my eyes. She was very thin; her shoulders could not withstand the howling wind. She looked mournful, but her eyes were tender and brilliant like black jade.

I knew I guessed correctly. "Sleep, she had a dream. Now she has woken up, but she has no way to ask for your forgiveness. If you still love her, go find her. You will both be liberated."

"I have to think about it," Sleep said. I knew he needed to digest everything I said.

Think about it, Sleep. These days, love is not simple and easy. It requires understanding, patience, and willpower. It has never been simple sweet enjoyment or innocent miracles. It is a cause; it is a cause that requires continued effort, endless sacrifice, and numerous payments of the heart. But you must be resolute. Because if she stood in the middle of your path tomorrow, you cannot avoid her.

Sometimes I feel Sleep and I are in a shower room. We

are both naked, not hiding anything. But the steam is thick, and neither can see the other clearly. We rely on the voice through the steam to prove the other is a few feet away.

I told him this analogy. Sleep was quiet for a moment, then said, "Really don't want to meet me? Of course I mean with clothes on."

I laughed. "No, I don't want to. Even if I wanted, I'm certain we would not."

"Fine." He sounded a bit unhappy. "Good night. Sweet dreams."

Sleep doesn't know, but he is like my pastor; his phone call is like my bedtime prayer. It calms down my chaotic senses and lets me sleep peacefully. With these, I no longer relied on wine or sleeping pills.

So much fog. Thick fog. Where is this? It seems to be a bridge. I approached hesitantly, and noticed someone on the bridge. He turned around and smiled at me. It's Jing, same as in the past. On our dates, he would stand in one spot with that expression on his face and watch as I walked up to him.

Jing! Wait for me! Take me away!

I flew into his arms. His embrace was cool. I said hold me tightly, I'm cold. Hold me tightly ...

But Jing opened his arms. He stared ahead, and his eyes lit up with tears.

What's wrong, I asked worriedly. He did not answer; he pushed me away, and left.

Jing! You cannot leave! If you leave me again, I will die! After I said this I suddenly realized Jing was already dead. I cried even more urgently, could you not leave? Stay with me for a moment, can you? Since you left, I have been very lonely. Have you not loved me, cared about me since you died? How could you?

Jing stood and turned his head; the fog lifted, and the moon shone. I saw tracks of tears on his face. He watched me and slowly shook his head, as if to refute what I said, as if to blame me for something, as if to beg desperately.

Jing! Don't go! Don't leave me by myself. I don't want to be by myself!

He continued to shake his head. He did not turn, but continued to watch me as he stepped backwards, backwards ... Seeing him approach the steps, I exclaimed: be careful! You'll fall down the steps!

He smiled at me and slowly took out something white from his pocket. He placed it on the railing, and stepped off the edge. He took one step, then immediately disappeared.

I desperately yelled: no!

I woke abruptly. In front of me there was no fog, no bridge; just the faint light through the blinds. I opened the blinds and was caught off guard to see a full moon hanging in the sky. The trees were half in clarity, half blurred. Not a shadow. Not a sound.

My mind was back, but my senses were jumbled. Tears dropped, like always. My heart contracted violently. My left temple throbbed.

What did Jing want to say to me? He should know everything about me. When he shook his head, was he disapproving of my current state? Or was he blaming me for an unreasonable request? He also cried, so it must be that he could not bear to leave me. The way he walked backwards, he wanted a few more glances of me. He even placed the white object on the railing.

I jumped up, put on some clothes, and ran out. I remembered. In front of the park, by the intersection, there is a bridge. I have to go see. What did Jing leave for me?

At the bridge, I ran up and found the corner where Jing disappeared. I saw a handkerchief on the railing, neatly folded, white. That's it. Jing left it for me before he left.

I took the handkerchief and held it tightly. It was damp. Was it dew, or was it … tears?

Jing, I understand. You are saying to me: dry your tears. Don't cry anymore. I understand. I understand completely. I hear you. You just have to come see me. It does not matter if it's here, or anywhere; you just have to appear, and I will go.

As soon as I got home, I called Sleep. My trembling fingers dialed his number. I did not hear it ring, but it sounded as if someone answered. I tested with a "hello," and his voice appeared. "Is it you?"

"Sleep, what happened?"

"I was dialing your number when I heard your voice."

"But I'm sure I dialed you first."

"Then we must've dialed at the same time, and answered at the same time," Sleep said.

"You know that's impossible. We should've heard busy signals." I said this, then paused. This unusual night, how could I still expect business as usual? Compared to what I have to tell him, what does it matter if our phones connected simultaneously?

"Sleep, let me tell you. I saw him!" I shouted.

Sleep listened to my whole story, sighed softly, then said, "You don't have to listen to other people. But don't you have to listen to him? Don't be sad anymore. You have cried long enough."

"Sleep, you believe me? You don't think I'm drunk, or I imagined all of it?" I couldn't believe it.

"The handkerchief is in your hand. Why not believe it? Dry that handkerchief, return it to him, and let him know you're not crying anymore. Only when you are good can he be saved." Sleep's voice is so mild and dense, like micro electricity circulating through my body.

I hung up and sat silent in my bed. I stared at the moon in the sky—so clear, so cool, with an endless tenderness.

Under its watchful gaze, I took off my clothes, and let it shine transparently through me.

I put the handkerchief on my chest, and dried it with the heat from my body.

As for Sleep's girlfriend, he later admitted to me: what I said was right, and other possibilities are harder to explain. I said it's not a question of explaining anything, it's about whether you accept it or not. To explain is rational; to accept is emotional. A lot of things that can be rationally explained cannot be accepted. Other things, once accepted there's no need for explanation.

I added at the end: love is never having to explain.

Sleep said you said it very well, it's moving. He did not share his stance.

Since then we have not brought up the subject again. We also did not talk about Jing.

In a floating state of mind, autumn came.

The sun and the wind together brew up warm, dry air. The falling leaves bow out on curtain call on behalf of all the plants; their gesture is greater than the preceding performance. I used to believe: if I could choose the season to die in, it must not be autumn; it would leave me too nostalgic for life. I so love autumn. But now I think, in the face of the final major test of life, perhaps autumn is the most helpful season. Autumn after autumn in life, we learn about dying calmly and bidding farewell graciously. It might not be so bad to practice during one autumn.

Even more exciting is the sky. The clear azure sky is its true color, but is few and far in between in city life. Pay attention and you'll see a mysterious smile amidst its candid face.

A heart that has been floating erratically suddenly quiets down.

Perhaps it is not the season. It is because I started being social again. A month ago, I received an invitation for a school gathering. My classmates had organized our 10-year class reunion. On the invitation was a script written by our class president, Big Bear: "Ten years have passed. Let's get together! If you refuse to acknowledge you miss everyone else, then let me take the lead. I admit it!" Of course this beats an invitation from the school officials a hundred times. I almost did not hesitate and signed the response card. Big Bear has been out of the country for several years. Just to hear him made me realize: it has been so many years; I have actually been apathetic or even depressed. I don't know how to express myself anymore. I do not like my classmates very much; but after ten years' time, all is good. Besides, compared to the people and things we have encountered since, our old differences and contradictions are nothing.

The reunion was very lively; it made me a little dizzy. But the genuine warmth made me willing to put up with it. Big Bear mercilessly criticized me: "You're still by yourself! I wasn't here before, now I have to take care of you!" I laughed, "Don't get so used to being class president. How will you take care of me? Marry me?" Tracy overheard, and said, "Big Bear, get a divorce. I knew you cared about her, but you were always speechless. So sad!" I said to Big Bear, "Really? Aww. Half the girls from our class had a crush on you. How could someone like me compete? I always thought you liked Tracy. Who knew you guys didn't follow through?" Big Bear said, "You two better separate yourselves by the Pacific Ocean. As soon as you get together it's head-to-head! I spent so much effort mediating you two in the old days."

Meeting up with old classmates, we unwittingly reverted back to our old selves. The ten years that passed easily evaporated.

Exchanging phone numbers and addresses, I rebuilt relationships with several of them. In the end it is the same group from the beginning. We went to movies, dinners, coffees. The like-minded ones were still like-minded. The ones I didn't like, I still didn't like. Ten years is too short a time to change someone's nature.

After meeting several times, we discovered the past years were all eventful for everyone. There is divorce. Someone's girlfriend ran away with another man right before the wedding. There is near-death illness. Someone has been unemployed multiple times. Someone's business partner defrauded more than half the savings. Someone played the stock market and lost all the hard-earned money from working overseas ...

Surprisingly, everyone is thick skinned. No one committed suicide or became a monk. Contrarily, everyone put it all back in to live life with savor. The person who was unemployed multiple times, he got outrageously excited talking about his experience. He even fought for the check, and said, "'Past this village there might not be another shop.' I cannot guarantee I'll have cash in my pocket to pay next time!" Barrister Wang, recognized as "Mr. Rich" in our class, heard this and made a grand gesture of putting his Visa card back in his wallet, provoking a burst of laughter.

Being with old buddies, we might not be able to feel the same youth of the school days. But to be in a group that knows each other's true identities, we feel we have returned to an era when anything can be attempted and tolerated.

Is this the only way to be in a good mood to look around yourself? I discovered the city that I am in has changed drastically. The old familiar things have all disappeared. Upon close inspection, one can find vague traces of the "old" in the unfamiliar "new." The old restaurant, coffee shop, movie theater are all gone. New structures have taken over their original places. The streetlights are brighter than before; everywhere is brightly lit. Shops emit faint fragrances; this also did not exist before. I really suspected I had entered a different city. I could not believe all these years I've lived here, I had not noticed any of this. I might have shut down all my senses towards the city? Incredible.

On Sunday, we had an all-nighter watching DVDs at Barrister Wang's. In his new home theater, he had a 56-inch television, and an incredibly powerful Danish sound system; it was hard not to notice and appreciate it. After a violent quarrel, we decided on a show of hands to watch *Comrades: Almost a Love Story*, *Face Off*, *Legends of the Fall*, and *Sense and Sensibility*. His home has very sophisticated European sofas and lounge chairs. But none of us sat in them. We all sat on cushions on the floor, leaning on the sofas. After the movies, everyone spread themselves across the floor. Tracy said, "I swear, this next six months I will not watch another movie! I can't digest this!" I was wide-awake. Barrister Wang had really great coffee; so thick and rich, I drank cup after cup until I was full of energy. It's funny the others said this coffee wasn't any good; their taste has been ruined by Nestle instant coffee.

When I got home it was already 7 a.m. I could not sleep, so I called Sleep: "Good morning! This is your morning call!"

He said, "I woke up early. I'm working out."

"Really? Wow! Great, morning workout."

"Have to work out, I have to start supporting the family," he said. He sounded a bit embarrassed.

"What?" I did not understand.

"Getting ready to get married. You shouldn't be surprised. I convinced her, to give ourselves a chance."

"She agreed?" My reaction is back. I asked with great surprise.

"She agreed. Hey, I'm not so bad. When I'm sincere I can really move someone." Sleep regained his ease.

He resolved to put his problem together with

her problem in order to solve them together. This courage, this decisiveness, really impressed me. I know it's not as easy as he says.

"So what's next?"

"I will bring her here to my place, that way it's simpler. Her kid enrolls in kindergarten soon; we are coming up with a name. If you're interested, help give me ideas. Yes, it's a boy. He has a round head, he's really fun."

This phone call was like a bucket of water poured down onto my head. Every inch of my skin has been cleansed, every pore refreshed. I cannot tell if I'm excited or disappointed; my heart was subjected to an unexpected shock. Wasn't this a good ending? I should be happy for Sleep, proud even. But how do I feel?

Unknowingly, I had gotten used to our way of getting along. We have no restraints, we freely talk about everything. When I comforted him, advised him, I did not think his decision would affect me. Now I know.

That is, Sleep will belong to a woman. This is a good thing for the two of them and for the world. But for me?

The special things of the world do not last long. Why did I forget that? My relationship with Sleep was too special. It was inevitable, there's no way around it: "the way we are" is coming to an end. But no one asked me, are you ready?

Too sudden. Too fast.

"I'm not going to say it. You might laugh at me," Sleep said.

"Say it. I promise not to laugh." This is the truth. To hear him so excited, I did not have the heart to laugh. I couldn't laugh.

"We want to have a wedding. Originally I didn't want one. Now I feel we should have a grand wedding."

I understand his feeling. "That's great. Why would I laugh? Marriage requires formality; formality means not avoiding trouble. Seriously go through some trouble to appear solemn, so you don't regret it."

"I was thinking the same, especially for her."

"Have you picked a place?"

"Yes." Sleep said the name of a four-star, European style hotel. I've been there for coffee. The atmosphere is classical and refined, but also very comfortable. It's not too showy, and the service is good. Sleep really has good taste.

"You must have a lot going on. Sending invitations, picking the dress, plus finding a witness, best man, maid of honor, enough for you to stay busy."

"Not too busy. Both sets of parents have waited so many years, they can't wait to help. So we let them handle most of it."

After he said this, he sighed both helplessly and gratefully. Both of us were quiet. Not sure what to say. This is something that has never happened to us before.

"Dream, what are you thinking?"

"In today's world, everything is rushed, everything is a thrill. But to marry your first love, like you two, that is a true legend. You are amazing. If you two are not happy in marriage, then no one should ever get married. I wish you two happiness." Such a cliché. But I believe every person who says it feels it in his or her heart.

"Thank you! Whether I do it or not is my business. Happiness is in the hand of the Gods, it has nothing to do with us." There was no sadness in his tone, just a light steadfastness.

"Also, I will not be calling you. Your wife had a unique experience; she could be extra sensitive. I don't want her to be suspicious."

"Really? Hmm ... OK. You understand women better than I do anyway. Besides, I can call you."

In my heart, I sighed. If I will not be calling you, I also will not let you call me. I do not like the feeling of not disclosing anything publicly, or any one-sided relationship. But I do not need to say it now, in order to save his good mood. After all, having love and a family, having one fewer friend is not so unbearable.

"Sleep, you must focus on taking care of her, and her child. If you have anything to say, you should say it to her; allow her to grow in understanding you, and you in understanding her. It'll be impossible for us to talk anytime, and we will no longer have much to say like we do now."

"I guess not." Sleep seemed not to know what to do. There was silence, and the rustling sound of the phone signal. This sound, in the middle of the night, was like the wind chasing falling leaves at the far end of the street; at this moment it was like a long, thin, drawn out sigh.

"Time to hang up! You have a lot of things to

prepare. Oh right, have you bought the ring?"

"We're using the original one. We bought it together four years ago. I kept it the whole time."

"You're destined! I envy you two."

"Dream, I actually envy the person who will marry you in the future. You really are a wonderful woman." My sentimental nature seems to have infected Sleep.

"Thank you. I love to hear that. I must store it away; when my inferior complex strikes, I'll take it out to comfort myself. OK, time to hang up, stop holding on. We've talked for a while."

We said "see you."

See you? This is a linguistic error. We have never seen each other; even if we met we would not recognize each other. But we are already at farewell. Sleep, maybe you should give me a gift, to help me prove that I truly have known you, that we have kept each other company on so many nights. But, if we can no longer talk to each other, what gift can comfort me?

A melancholy rose from my heart, like a boat leaving the harbor but indefinitely mired in the water vapors.

The whistle blows. The boat departs, far, out of sight. Then the crowd on the pier leaves. There are no more silhouettes of people on the dock, even the dust has settled back on the ground. The water flows, like it has for thousands of years, without changing its sound or color. There is not a trace of the boat on the water surface. What just happened, a scene that seemed like it would continue, dissipates like the fog, as if it never happened.

But, there is always something left behind. The image in the eyes, the sound waves in the ear, the touch on the skin—when it's all gone, there is always something left behind. I am such a fool; that night I actually ran to the bridge to find what Jing had left behind. If I knew he came by, then he came by. Why do I need an object to prove it? If I still had doubt, then that handkerchief could have been dropped by a passerby. But I believed it was Jing, because I knew.

It's all in my heart. It's only gone if it has been resolved in the heart. Only regrets in the heart are meaningless, without resolution.

Today is Sleep's wedding day, so I did something good today, as my wedding gift to Sleep.

I typed up a letter on the computer. I told all my relatives, friends, classmates, I'm changing my phone number. I will not let Sleep find me, so when he's feeling weak or when he feels regret ... I know this will happen. If his wife cannot help him through everything, then he must face it alone. I can only wish him the best. There's nothing more I can do.

What I give is the best gift I can give—to disappear from his life, so he does not have an escape route.

Finally, I want to call him; this will be my last call to him. I only want to say to him my congratulations. But all I got was an automatic voice message: "Sorry, the number you have dialed has changed." I was surprised and dialed again, but I stopped midway.

I paused, then laughed. Sleep and I are just too much alike—so sensitive, so resolute. I am not even sure if we know each other too well, or if we do not trust each other; we actually made the exact same decision, with the same swiftness. Now, even I do not have an escape route; it is too late for regret. What Sleep and I wanted were the same. We knew we were not strong enough, would regret at any moment, and might ruin it all. So we made it impossible for the other to regret.

The phone number is our bridge. Now the bridge is broken. Or, we used to have a password, but the password has changed. He will never find me again, and I will never find him again. From now, we return to being two unrelated pieces of dust in this city, floating, never meeting.

After work, after everyone left the office, I stayed. I did not want to go home, nor did I want to go out. I was not sad, nor was I frustrated. I just did not want to see anybody. This day, I just want it to be mine only.

My office is on the 23th floor. During the day, it looks out to building roofs and busy streets. It's aggravating. At night, when the mess is out of sight, and the hustle and bustle has died down, everything lights up. All the homes and buildings become lit up like lanterns. It all becomes pretty. The buildings with floodlights look like evening beauties, flirtatious, smiling. The whole city turns into an ocean of light. No, the whole city is a beautiful woman, with her eyes brilliant and clear, flowing to and fro.

I have never seen this beautiful night view. Maybe it is because I am alone in the dark, without the lights on.

I remember going on trips with Jing. Looking down from the top of the mountain, the city lights are exceptionally bright. Jing said each light is a family, a world of their own. They do not feel they are in the light, but only those in the dark can see it clearly. To view lights, one must be in the dark. I do not remember which mountain it was. What I do remember, clearly, are Jing's words and his expressions when he said them.

I am watching the lights from the dark.

I know that for Jing, who is far away, I am also a bright light. He is in an even darker place; he can see things clearer than everyone else. If I am left in this light, I must take extra care to keep my light on, so he can see me, smiling back at him. As for our reunion, there is no rush. That date has been set.

I went downstairs, and slowly walked out of the office building. The streets of autumn are filled with the aroma brewed from spring and summer. Couples escape air conditioning and stroll on the streets in pairs. The sound of a saxophone floated far and wide. A gust of wind tossed my hair to cover my eyes. In that moment, not being able to see anything, a clear empty space appeared in my mind. The space was cool, without a speck of dust. It is like everything has happened, and anything can happen, whether for me, or for this world.

Walking aimlessly, I passed by a flower shop and saw half a bucket of tea roses by the front door. The shop keeper smiled and asked, "Miss, buy some flowers. At night they don't look as vibrant as morning glory. In fact, these are very fresh." I said I would take it all; she said, "Oh, miss, you're so straightforward. I'll give you a discount. Come again next time." She glanced at me again. "You're not married yet. We do pre-order bridal bouquets and hair pieces. When you get married, come to my shop and choose to your heart's content!"

I never imagined I would be associated with this topic. But this is a common blessing for a girl. Why bother pursuing it? I said, "Great. What discount will you give me?"

The shop lady pondered, looked at me again, and decisively said, "Half price! Consider it making a new friend."

"Then I must thank you in advance!" Now we are just saying it, but it might actually come true in the future. In life, there are many things—you plan them and they fail; you don't plan them but they come to fruition. Actually, expected or unexpected, it is all a delusion. In the laws of nature, everything is predictable; nothing is ever missed.

Walking out of the shop holding a big bouquet of roses feels completely different. The fragrance rushes to my face softly; from the shop continuously to where I stood it surrounds me. The wind tosses my hair and mixes with the floral scent. A few pedestrians looked at me. They must have thought I was going on a date. Such a wonderful illusion. I almost believed it myself.

I was almost home when my footsteps changed direction. I walked onto the bridge, and placed the flowers on that particular step. I thought for a bit, and took out the white handkerchief from my pocket, placing it on the flowers. I did not know if Jing would still visit. I also did not know if he could take this gift. But I was willing to do this. I knew he would understand. I trusted him, as he continued to trust me.

There's a communication that will never be shaken, never change. Only those who have unwavering belief in this deserve to live in this world, can survive in this world.

My two hands are empty again, but the fragrance remains, except it is in traces, intermittent strands. I walked away leisurely, at a brisk pace. Another passerby gave me a glance. Why? I don't have flowers in my hands anymore. Then I realized: I was smiling.

A woman walks along at night with fragrance on her hands and a smile on her face. No one knows what is on her heart. There is no need to know. Looking up, the color of the sky grew increasingly peaceful. Above my head, in all directions, the night is smiling back at me. We understand each other.

For countless nights into the future, there will no longer be a familiar voice for us to slowly take in. We will hear a lot of other, unknown voices, some sweet, some not. Or there will be nothing.

I will sit in stillness. The purpose is not to be silent, but rather to speak to myself. I will not refuse to listen. I will listen to the night.

Stories by Contemporary Writers from Shanghai